Civilized Blacks

Free American Negroes in the 1870's
Whose Lives Paralleled the Life of Booker T. Washington

by

Carol Binta

DORRANCE
PUBLISHING CO
EST. 1920
PITTSBURGH, PENNSYLVANIA 15222

Dorrance Publishing Co
701 Smithfield Street
Pittsburgh, PA 15222
Visit our website at www.dorrancebookstore.com

ISBN: 978-1-4809-0900-7
eISBN: 978-1-4809-0762-1

Dedication

To my daughters, I and I, 326;

we are one under the Gemini sun II.

Acknowledgments

I'd like to acknowledge all my girlfriends who helped with the editing and review of this work. You know who you are. I would be remiss in not also thanking my daughters, who missed me when I was in "Alabama," as they used to tell callers, even though I was just in the next room.

The family portrayed on the cover is a real family that comes very close to representing the period of time that the novel is placed. Thomas Hunter Amos, school principal, and Ida Brock Amos, science teacher, are pictured in the lower left amongst other teaching staff. Their descendants were kind enough to lend me the portrait.

I will be forever grateful for the opportunity I had to meet with a member of another real family, Mother Hunt, whose ancestor I discovered while researching the historical chronology of the period in the novel. It was a tremendous experience to meet Mother Hunt in Sparta, Georgia. I won't tell the story here, but the fictional character in this novel closely resembles a real-life figure named Adele Hunt who worked close to Booker T. Washington during the early days of the Tuskegee Institute. On a trip to Sparta, I was fortunate enough to encounter the great-great-granddaughter of Adele Hunt and her mother, the great-granddaughter. Before the writing of this work, I had not known anything of them or their ancestors. This is what was amazing. Meeting them was a confirmation of the fiction's historical accuracy. Although I had no prior knowledge of them, I had tapped into a soul remembrance in creating this narrative. I would like to express gratitude to both of them for their cordiality and interest in my work. Mother Hunt was 106 when I visited her in Sparta.

Finally, I thank my own ancestors, especially for giving me my mother, who insisted on excellence in thought, word, and deed. Thank you, Nana, my great-grandmother, for being able to write, read volumes, and speak so eloquently from the pulpit. She was born in 1872 and was my first spiritual guide until she died in 1967. Thanks Grandmother Dutton. Your example of quiet determination helped me a lot during this journey. Thanks to Uncle Ray for his faith in me. Moreover, I honor the spirit that is in every writer, dancer, songwriter, vocalist, painter, poet, and prayerful person for it is holy and truly worthy of praise.

Introduction

Civilized Blacks is a historical fiction about a young girl named Pansy Outlaw, her family, and her dream to become a scientist. Her odd friendship with Huckabuck Marie is almost her only source of encouragement until she meets the ultimate mentor. The two young Negro women have no regard for the limits placed upon them in the late nineteenth century's rural South. They are fortunate to meet an educator, Mr. Washington, during the time he is laying the foundation for an agricultural and trade school in their town. Though completely opposite to each other, they mutually benefit from his appearance in the spectrum of their lives. Pansy is destined to pursue a teaching career, and Huckabuck Marie is offered an opportunity to work at the new school. The three of them interact in and about the Outlaw household, establishing a lasting bond based on mutual respect and appreciation amidst the lavishness of well-to-do Negro, down-home, Southern style hospitality.

Unlike the Ebonics of today, the broken English spoken by these turn-of-the-century free Negroes was a testimony to an irreversible spiritual quest for excellence. Language was a simple adaptation from a native tongue along with the preservation of certain phonics. The real challenge awaited those in the new millennium where generations of Negroes would, during the process of learning perfect English, be duped into forgetting the language styles and heritage of their ancestors.

"Civilized" refers to a mastery over the social nomenclature of their time. Nomenclature: (no men kla tur), n. [Lat. <no-men, name+calare, to call] 1. The collection of words and terms, or the system of names for things, used in any art or science; as, the system used in a specific branch of learning or activity. What a total joy for me to remember those Civilized Blacks who never forgot and yet were able to master their new turf.

Chapter I

Remembrance

Luke didn't have a clue who his real pappy was, and I wasn't about to tell him now. That is the kinda stuff you tell folk when the sun is risin', birds are chirpin', and the day is fresh. Now, cuz the sun was meltin' on the west and dusk was creepin' over us, I'd be quiet 'bout dat. It was evenin', and as the sun slowly set beneath the horizon, the heat of the long hot summer day was rollin' backward like flood waters after the rain. Across the tobacco field you could see for miles into the shimmerin' sunset. Leaves were dancin' in the sun. The black of the night was comin', and there'd be plenty of creatures of the dark crawlin' out—safe from the predators who roamed the sky. No need to bring the dark of folk's life out too. A long silence cloaked the drawin' room from the high arched ceilings to the bottom of heavy brocade drapes hanging just above the tobacco road red acacia hardwood floors. Luke stood tall and slender, red boned with chocolate overtones in his vested suit and leather strapped-up shoes. He was holding his corn cob pipe lost in thought by the fireplace.

"I'm the memory," announced Pansy Outlaw, as though continuin' a conversation that was going on inside her.

Boy! She is loud, thought Luke, as her sudden announcement startled him back into awareness of her presence.

"Look out over this sprawlin' land," she continued. "This is it, the 'ole Judd Outlaw's plantation. Most of you black folks don't even want to remember. Not me, my past was sweet like cherry muscatel. I get drunk from it too, sometime, and pass out. Then, when the mornin' come, my life is sweet again. I tell yah, whenever it rains, I'm the one can see the flowers hidin' in the clouds."

"Aunt Pansy! Be careful leaning back in that rickety ole' rocking chair," Luke warned.

"No need to worry about me or the chair. You just stand there across the room lookin' pretty. Sides, boy, don't you know some things just get better with time, like this here rockin' chair? Take a good look at it, chile. Sure, it squeaks a little, but it's one of the strongest pieces of cultured wood in all of Granville County, Alabama. Can't nobody carve curves like this no more!"

"Nobody but the Lord," Luke agreed. He shamefully recalled the succulent figure of his Aunt Pansy back in the days when her curves could make a sick mule walk.

"Luke, I declare, you sho' a sight for sore eyes standin' there. I hope you listenin' too. Can I tell you how many hundreds of famous dinners were cooked in that hearth? While you restin' your elbow on that mantle, just think about that for a while. Imagine six kettles hangin' from it 'stead of yo' tall lean body gracin' the opening to that 'ole red brick hearth. And 'stead of yo' puffs of cigarette smoke, the smell of smoked turkey was risin' in there. I'm smellin' tobacco right now, but I'm thinkin' turkey!"

"I don't' believe I can remember back that far," Luke said. "I do remember one thing."

I was wonderin' what his 'ole devilish mind was thinking up now. His great-great-grandfather was Judd T. Outlaw, known throughout Granville for his ability to retain the oral history from five generations before him. His great-grandfather Judd Outlaw ran the Outlaw farm and mansion like a landlord with silver dollars growing in the fields. His grandfather, Li'l Luke Outlaw, his namesake, had every postal route memorized with the exact delivery times for each stop in town by the time he was twelve years old. The only daddy he knowed commanded a regiment of one hundred soldiers and knew the names of every one of them. So I don't know who he thinks he's foolin'.

"So you do remember one thing, eh? I wonder what that would be."

"Well, er…it's kinda hard to describe," stuttered Luke.

"Well, if it's about this ole' rocker, I can tell ya, this rocker has Outlaw butt prints engraved in the seat forever."

"Precisely," Luke replied, "and some are permanently etched in my mind."

"And look at you, Luke, smellin' up this room same like yo' granddaddy and yo' great granddaddy used to. You're smokin' the same nasty smellin' stuff too. Now your granddaddy, he was the quiet type who could look you straight in the eye while he was liftin' your pocket watch. Your great-great-granny, Mama Tutu, can rest in peace for all the times she pinched your granddaddy's ears. And you, you really could make sore eyes heal. You, dear boy, are the substance of things hoped for."

"I suppose, Auntie, that that is a good thing?" Luke questioned.

"Good? It's more than good, boy. It's holy. It's livin' proof that can't no evil tempest stop the marchin' forward of a family rooted in tradition and leanin' on de Lawd. Sure as you da' one standin' there fo' me, I ain't got a reason to doubt. I could bust right out cryin' just lookin' at ya. You the image of yo' granddaddy, and he's the one who stole my heart way before life got complicated. Now he done come back to me through you."

"Hmm..." Luke responded still looking a little uncertain.

"What's on yo' mind, boy?" I asked.

"Oh, nothing."

"Don't tell me nothin'. I didn't just meet ya', you know."

"No, really, I'm quite fine."

Luke stirred the tobacco in his pipe and struck a stick match on the sole of his shoe. Holding the flame over the pipe's bowl, he puffed and blew until the crimson fluorescent leaves regained their kindle. He started walking back and forth, blowing and puffing. He stopped and stared blankly into the open hearth.

"I know it's somethin', Luke. Why don't you give yo' granny aunt a shot at it?"

Then Luke turned to me and said, "I have everything a man could want, Aunt Pansy, everything, and only one thing stands between me and the state legislature."

"And what's that?" I asked.

"My skin is black."

"Heeee heeee.... I done heard it all now. Yo' skin is...huh? And what did you expect it to be? Yo' daddy, granddaddy, and great-granddaddy's skin was black. So, I hope you wasn't hoping for somethin' else? Truth is, boy, if I sat here with my eyes closed and I was holdin' you in my lap, I sho nuff wouldn't know that you was black. Trouble with you is you ain't black enough. And let me tell you somethin'. Being black ain't got nothin' to do with the color of yo' skin."

Yes suh, that really got to me. I couldn't believe what I had just heard. My back stiffened, and I straightened right up in that 'ole rocker. My left hand automatically landed on my hip and with my elbow perched on my right knee; I flung out my pointer finger aimed right between his eyes. He looked ready to duck.

"Okay, you want to know somethin' about black. Let me tell you somethin' about black! I know me a man who was as yella as the sun and to top it off he had a head full of red hair. To this day ain't no man alive, east or west of the Mississippi can look his own dark black face in a mirror and be mo' black than he. I still remember that first day I met him, like it was dis very mornin'."

That day the sun was barely peekin' above the horizon, streaks of purple-rose light was streamin' through the kitchen window giving a splatter of color to Mama Tutu's white apron. She stood waist high at the butcher block choppin' ingredients for the cornbread stuffin'. Shortly, she would be stuffin' it into her freshly killed fowl. She had already made butter from the mornin' skim and it was sizzlin' in the skillet. The fire was cracklin' kinda slow, but that open hearth where you standin' was gonna be roarin' by the time the sun was midway across the sky. By then, Mama Tutu would be as cool as a Black Madonna on the road from Jerusalem to Bethlehem! I mean she could handle anythin' in the dinner preparation field. That mornin' though, uh-huh, she was wipin' the sweat from her brow with the tail of her apron.

That was the first day we was hostin' the new schoolmaster, 'cause ours was the biggest house in the congregation. He was gonna build a new school. We were all excited. We wanted to make the best impression we could on him. Mama Tutu always said it was the first impression that was most important. She sent for Jasper Ale just to polish the family silver dinner service. In her mind he was less than dirt, a lowlife who just happened to be a historian because of his love for gossip and stickin' his nose in Outlaw business. He'd be snoopin' around anyway, so might as well give him somethin' to do. That he did. He spent the whole night polishin' 'til mornin'. I was lookin' on from the top of the stairs. We had a set of stairs that led to the kitchen and another set of stairs that flowed down into the foyer like a giant water fall of royal blue, green, and copper colored carpets of a Persian floral design. He was handlin' them silver pieces like they were part of the lost Ark of the Covenant. He was always tryin' to impress Mama Tutu in hopes that one day he could come up to snuff. The truth is there wasn't a chance that one day Mama Tutu would ever warm up to Jasper Ale. The silver had been in the family for five generations and shined like new with a little touch up. There wasn't a polish in Granville that could clean Jasper Ale up enough for Mama Tutu though.

"This adds my name to the family tree," Jasper Ale said.

"If polishing silver was what it took to be an Outlaw, we wouldn't have a family tree. You lucky I'm letting you touch 'em, Jasper Ale," Mama Tutu said with a scowl.

Mama Tutu was proud of our family and only took out the silver for special occasions. The rest of the time she hid it. You would think anyone could polish silver, but she had to make Jasper Ale, the town historian, do hers.

"Make sure you get in between the detailed pattern on the handle."

"Yes, ma'am," he answered her, just like a child.

Deacon Brown stopped by most Sunday mornings, for a biscuit or two and also just to make sure we knew that it was Sunday mornin'. Pastor Smith assigned him to remind us eva' week that, as model Christians, we were expected to be on the front row of the church. That Sunday mornin' the Reverend Smith had also come by personally to ask Papa if our family would host the welcomin' reception for the new schoolmaster when he arrived. Mama Tutu was way ahead of the reverend and was in the midst of puttin' together a feast of all feasts.

"Dey tell me General Armstrong is sendin' us the best black man ta ever come up from Hampton," said Mama Tutu.

She was primpin' a huge turkey that had been soakin' like an Egyptian princess in spices all night long. She stuck her hand inside the bird to size up just how many onions she should be choppin' for her famous stuffin'. I heard her laughin' out loud sayin' to Jasper Ale, "Why do we call such a delicious bird fowl and some fool like you is called a historian?"

"That shows how much you know. It's come down from Hampton," Jasper Ale said with a smirk of ire, not even bothering to answer the question about the fowl.

"And he ain't nothin' but somebody done tried so hard to be white that the General might as well be sendin' his very own shadow. He bedn' not come down here thinkin' weez trying to be lak dat, 'cause the only thing we 'no fo' sure is, if de white man like him, den we won't," Jasper Ale scoffed with indignation.

Right then your grand-papa, Lil' Luke, come bustin' right in on the conversation. Nobody even remembered he was in the room. Mama Tutu had kept him busy countin' the silver.

"Whoever he is, Uncle Jasper, I ain't seen this much fuss made over nobody that was still livin'. Can you, 'majun Mr. Washington's po' belly after he gets through eatin' all 'dem dumplin's and 'tada pies waitin' for him on every farm? He gonna' scratch his head and flop down in Papa's ole rocker and wish that General Clay had sent the army 'stead of him." Lil' Luke then commenced to laughin' and makin' faces, rubbin' his hand over his stomach. "This is how he'll look like after two stops," he continued, blowin' his cheeks up like a balloon. Lil' Luke usually thought he was a lot funnier than others thought him to be and he was fallin' out laughin' when Mama Tutu spoke up again.

"Now don't you get your mind off countin' them silver pieces, Lil' Luke," she scolded.

"We might have to send Pansy out to rustle up the missin' pieces, if there are any that walked off. Nobody brings nothin' back round here, so it's yo' job to make sure they is all here."

"How many sets of five you 'spose to have, boy?" she asked.

"There are eight sets of five, Mama T."

"That's right, that's right. And how many does that equal, boy?"

Lil' Luke got busy counting each set by fives.

"It's uh…five, ten, fifteen…forty, Mama T, forty pieces of silver!"

"That 'a boy, Lil' Luke. Did you hear that, Jasper Ale? My boy gonna get free 'mission to de Normal School when it's his time to go. I do declare he done got his gran' Mammy's skill wit de numbers."

"Some folks call it skill," said a jeering Jasper Ale, "and others call it wheelin' and dealin'!" He screamed that lookin' back as he scrambled toward the door so to avoid any spoon that may have come flyin'.

I was lappin' up the kitchen conversation like a pup does a warm bowl of milk. I didn't want to miss the endin' so I ran through the upstairs hallway to the top of the main staircase just in time to hear Mama Tutu.

"Now, Jasper Ale," Mama Tutu yelled after him, "just 'cause I got a better price on dem brood sows you sold me last month, you ain't whinin' is you?"

Jasper Ale just waved his hand and shouted back at Lil' Luke, "See you in church, boy. If you gonna folla' your Mama T's 'sample, you betta' get all the prayin' in now while you is still young!"

Lil' Luke just kept grinnin' at himself.

"Unlike you, with your face always twisted up in knots, your granddaddy never had a worried thought in his head."

"Ah tell ya, Luke, I kin remember like it was yesterday. 'Bout the time he was finishin' up, I was sneakin' down the stairs in my nightshirt. I noticed he could see me from the bottom of the stairs, I quickly turned around and haul tailed it back up dem steps like a rabbit runnin' from a fox. 'Don't mind me— I'm leavin',' he yelled. 'I'm better off in the path of wild horses than in your Mama T's pantry.' I kin remember him wavin' goodbye. 'A pleasant good morning to you, Missus Pansy,' he said. He hurried down the porch steps and walked briskly toward the main road."

"I can tell this is going to be a long one," Luke said. Luke wasn't really all that interested in family history, even though he was the third Luke on the Outlaw family tree. He just sneered and walked toward the window and stared out at the ivy twistin' its way up the columns like the winding road stretched out across the tree lined entrance to the estate. Just as Judd Outlaw's stately Southern farmhouse was Luke's inheritance, understandin' his legacy was clearly my mission. I started back in on the story.

Back then, Granville was the kind of Southern town that did not have a lot of industry, and so money was scarce. However, there was never any shortage on hospitality at our house. The white town folk called the road to our house Thousand Mile Road, 'cause it was a road well-trodden with thousands of miles of footprints. Mama Tutu and the other Negro neighbors often shared the finer things they had with each other. Jasper Ale was always tryin' to cash in on the benefits of our family. After all, we were among the fortunate few. Our house was so vibrant and enticin', especially that day when Mr. Washington was comin'. I was so anxious to help out.

"What can I do, Mama Tutu?" I asked.

"Make sure all the plates and servin' bowls are spotless, and before you do, check in the cupboard to make sure they is all here," she said.

It was nothin' for Mama Tutu to send a bowl of greens or 'tatas home with someone after havin' guests for dinner. Plates, cups, bowls, and servers were lined up neatly behind the shinin' glass doors of the polished wooden oak china closet. We appreciated antiques and imported finery; we also knew their value and how to use them. As soon as I was downstairs Lil' Luke started in again.

"I bet Miss Margaret be cookin' one of her best cherry pies," he said.

"She heard tell that he like cherry pies, and I know why she is tryin' to impress him. 'Cause she hopes maybe he'll take all of them hell raisin' chillun of hers into his school. She been praying the same prayer every week for months at prayer meetin'," he continued.

Right then, I just got in my feelin's and I was gettin' ready to say somethin' when Mama Tutu spoke first.

"Oh, hush up, Lil' Luke," she said. "You know you ain't s'pose ta be tellin' what you hear dem women sayin' at 'da prayer meetin's. Go on, if you done go on and get."

Knowin' better than to be told twice, Lil' Luke scooted out the back door. He knew what was next. So to avoid a serious ear pinchin', he ran out of the house and kept on around the house, slidin' his hand along the white painted railings enclosin' the porch. Plants hung lavishly from the beams overhead around the ornately trimmed borders. Lil' Luke liked to hang out on the front porch in the mornin's. Sometimes he'd get lucky and Miss Huckabuck Marie be traipsin' through our estate on the short-cut to the post office. She was the controversial town floosy who could walk down the street with a swagger in her rump that could make a homeless man happy. For Lil' Luke, it was his first crush on an 'older women.' She wasn't really old though, only to him. To me, she was my best friend, but to every other woman in town, she was the devil. The men, when they wasn't tryin' to take her for a fool, mostly feared her like the plague. Lil' Luke was too young and too dumb to be afraid and continuously plotted ways to have a glimpse of her.

Mama Tutu coaxed me over to the breakfast table with a bowl of porridge and began to speak about all the changes in Granville. I musta been a good soundin' board because half the time I didn't know what she was talkin' about. She told me she was sure the town's people wasn't gonna like no changes. So since Mama Tutu was one of the most influential persons in town, I think she thought it was her personal responsibility to persuade the people of Granville to just be willin' to give him a chance. She told me all about her hope for the new school and how it would benefit all of Granville's children for many years to come. We continued talkin' for a little while until she noticed that she didn't hear Lil' Luke makin' any noise out back. When she looked out of the back door for him, he wasn't there.

"Humph! That little rascal is slippery as silver fish," she said.

She stomped across the kitchen floor through the parlor to the front door and there he was hangin' out in front hopin' and waitin'.

"Come on, Lil' Luke, get yo'se'f on in here 'fo dat 'ole Huckabuck Marie come paradin' down the street," screamed Mama Tutu. "'Cause if yo' daddy come ta look out for you round dis time when she usually be sashayin' pass heah, you know yo' mamma sure ain't gonna like dat. She be thinkin' for certain that he da one be lookin' out for huh and not you. 'Den weez be up all da night wit' dey's hollerin' and bangin' 'round stuff. Eva' time dat chile' pass by heah der's trouble gonna follah, 'ole scratch be nippin' at huh heals," she grumbled.

The next thing I knew, Mama Tutu, with no warnin', grabbed Lil' Luke by the ear and swung him around the old splintery wood screened door. I could hear that door clappin' back and forth for five minutes 'til it went back to hangin' slightly off-kilter in that wide country door frame. Yes suh, that was how it was the day he came.

Chapter II

Judd Outlaw's House

When everyone got home from church, the whole congregation was talkin' about the new school.

"More Negroes will be able to work when they learn the new way to make bricks," Jasper Ale said as Mama Tutu prepared for dinner.

"I ain't knowed you could even say the word work," snickered Mama Tutu.

"All you ever did was repeatin' somethin' somebody else already done and call it history."

"Somebody gotta keep a record of this mess you call family," he responded with a good amount of irritation.

"Jasper Ale, tie yuh mout' fo' you be swallowin' yuh foot!" Mama Tutu exclaimed.

Our house filled up after church like it was the second worship service. Soul food was the menu and the news about anyone and everyone was the preached word. Still dressed in their church clothes and hats, the faithful of Granville piled up on the porch, around the porch, and down the front steps, all waitin' to taste Mama Tutu's scrumptiously prepared Sunday dinner. Children scattered around the grounds playin' hide and seek while folks got together like long lost relatives catchin' up on the news, chatterin' like bees buzzin' 'round a honeycomb and sometimes continuin' the sermon in their own words. Deacon Brown was sportin' his white on white in white hat, suit, shirt, socks, and shoes. The ladies were in full bloom in every color of the rainbow. They marched up the footpath swingin' dey handbags with shoes in matchin' complimentary colors. Men naturally gathered on one side and women on the other. Papa usually pulled out his checkers and beat one after the other while he talked. He had memorized every offensive and defensive move there was and no one in the congregation had ever won a game with him. The men hunched over the checker board in full attention while he sized up the situation about the comin' of the new schoolmaster.

"I know that if farmin' down here improves like it did for the Virginia farmers, after they started usin' his new soil fertilizer" said Papa before makin' his move, "then money gonna be rainin' down on Granville."

"Why, I heard even white men is travelin' all 'da way from across the state to buy his homemade bricks," Deacon Brown said.

Papa smiled with confidence and added, "They sayin' 'dem bricks is harder and stronger than any brick in the Union."

"Anybody come all the way down heah, shoot, they'll buy 'em, whatever the price," Jasper Ale chuckled. "Bricks sellin' and 'mo produce growin', Granville Negroes will see freedom come in the black instead of in the red."

Hidden from the porch company behind the densely draped windows was a huge feast in preparation. Silver platters and china dinnerware adorned the eloquently decorated mahogany table. The immense dinin' hall was outlined with a tall antique china closet behind the head of the table and long twin hutches on either side in matchin' mahogany. If you sat as straight as an oak tree, your head would still not reach over the top of the backs of the dinin' room chairs. The cushions were lush with satin ribbons woven in between the fabric. Lil' Luke used to try ever so hard to count the crystal drops hangin' from the chandelier and would always get dizzy lookin' up for so long and lose count. My favorite thin' used to be the tiffany lamps around the room that would cast a kaleidoscopic of colors all over the taffeta wallpaper.

Right after Papa blessed the food before dinner, the talk continued. "We on our way now," Papa said. "I reckon this chap Washington is worth his weight in gold. And gold is what this town Granville is fixin' to have by the barrels. I don't know much about schoolin', but if the government sent all the way up to Virginia for this fella, you know he ain't up there just whistlin' Dixie. How the hell somebody thinks you can learn farmin' in school is beside me, but eva'body's singin' his praises, like he 'da second comin' of the Lawd. He must be slicker than a Saturday night preacher to hear folks talk about him."

"He's a teacher, Papa, he ain't no preacher," a small voice piped up, interruptin' the grown folks talk.

A sudden hush fell over the room. All eyeballs around the table shifted. Their focus was jarred away from 'tadas, greens, macaroni, and slices of roast beef and cast on me like an iron lung wrapped around a body paralyzed with polio. In Judd Outlaw's house everybody would'a known betta' than to interrupt Papa when he was talkin'. That was an Outlaw law, and it applied to man, woman, and child. If you were a man, you could easily be shot for somethin' like that. Jasper Ale had seen Papa pull a pistol on his own brother one Sunday mornin' after church over the same kinda slip. One day Papa gave a woman, who tried to cut him off, orders to, "Remember who you are, gal, and mind your tongue."

I had gotten caught up in the excitement of the moment. Mama Tutu used to warn me, "You forgettin' yo'sef, chile," when my mouth ran ahead of my mind that way. A child, like me, shucks, would usually simply get the back of his hand across the mouth. But that day, he diverted his attention to Lil' Luke and said, "You go on upstairs and get some of that red Alabama dust out of your ears, boy." Motionin' to me, he said, "Mind after your brother, chile, and when you done prayin' his prayers with him, come on down and help yo' mamma."

'Yes, suh,' I said, and quickly excused myself from the table.

Den he went right back to the conversation.

"As I was sayin', we Negroes is gonna be free, free at last. Weez already freed from slavery, now we goanna' be free of our pitifully helpless and hopeless future. I may not live to see it, but I got my bets on 'ole yella!" he shouted, referrin' to Washington's light skin.

'Wit eva'body holdin' they breath, still fearin' the worst, I knew I had narrowly escaped with my life. It was not because of the company, neither. Company never stopped Papa Judd. Perhaps, it was because I was Pansy. I was lucky to be one of his favorites. Even so, hardly a day passed without my papa and me lockin' horns. I remember another time I was fixin' some new saplin's in the soil around the side of the house. Papa and Deacon Brown were sittin' on the porch playin' checkers. Deacon Brown used to come in between Sundays so he could have a better chance of winnin' one day. Deacon Brown was explainin' to Papa why he thought the pastor was goin' to ask him to host the new schoolmaster. "You are the most prestigious family in the community," he said. "I am sure he's gonna pay a handsome ransom for your service."

Papa was countin' the days of the week on his hand from Sunday to two Wednesdays from then. I jumped in the conversation and said, "That's not fair, Papa. He's gonna need all the money he can muster up to start the new school!" Papa slammed the checker down on the board, stood up, turned around, and propped one foot on top of the railin' in a very threatenin' stance.

"And who in tarnation asked you for your opinion on the matter, Miss Pansy?" he shouted.

I tried to explain. "It's just that I've been readin' about the new school plans in the farmer's almanac and—"

"Mind your beeswax and hush up before I lose my temper," he replied.

"Did I say anythin' about chargin' him, Deacon Brown?" he asked.

See Papa had a way of makin' it seem like he wasn't payin' any attention to me or that I was too young and imprudent to be taken seriously. The truth is he did listen to me and was sometimes embarrassed by how much sense I really made. This was especially true in front of his peers who imagined him with absolute power and authority.

Sunday dinner was a popular meetin' place at the Outlaw homestead. After services, several of the church members would follow Papa's carriage back home to sit on the big porch and drink ice-cold lemonade. Don't think just anybody could come. You had to be somebody. Either you were a teacher, a preacher, or somethin' important. While I's be graciously servin' the guest fresh-squeezed lemonade, I'd be takin' a head count and runnin' numbers back to the kitchen. Mama Tutu's Sunday dinner was as sacred as the mornin' service, and from my head count, she would know to throw a few more 'tadas into the stew. Papa used to lean back in the 'ole rocker and study the face of each person as I served them the drink. I didn't know then, but he trusted nobody with his pride and joy. Not even church folk. He'd be makin' sure that ain't no funny looks go between me and some of them deacons, what had big reputations wit' da gals around town. I was only twelve years old, but since this was the first year of 'mancipation, some of the church men thought they could now act like white men with the fresh young chickens, if you know what I mean.

"Look at my beautiful spring flower," he'd say, pointin' at me with the mouthpiece end of his pipe. "Any bee get close to huh and they'll be hummin' in paradise, and that's if they lucky."

Deep down inside he worried though, wit my bein' outspoken by nature. He also knew me and knew that I had about as much interest in house chores, havin' babies, or takin' care of them as a cow has in playin' checkers. I was real at ease in the company of the men at these afternoon discussions and, accordin' to Papa, it concerned him that I was not attracted to the kitchen where the women gathered. On the other hand he was proud of me and he liked me bein' around him and the men. I didn't even mind that servin' them was the only accepted way of bein' in their midst.

Lil' Luke was the only chile I cared anythin' about. I loved yo' papa just like he was my own son. I can see him now runnin' up and down that huge set of stairs like a rabbit in a cabbage patch. I reckon if dem stairs could talk, they'd be live in the porch gossip with the stories they could tell. They heard Mama and Papa talk about things us chillun' couldn't hear. And Lawd knows Mama Tutu never held her tongue goin' or comin'. There was so much about her that was a deep dark secret. Oh, those steps could tell it all, but they just sat there witnessin' the joys and the pains that played out in their presence.

The same Sunday night that the schoolmaster came to town, I came as close to gettin' slapped by Papa as I ever did. I was takin' Lil' Luke up dem same stairs over there for his night bath. We counted each step as we went, and he cheerfully hopped one by one to the count. He was still so small he had to jump onto each step. By the time we reached the top, he turned his lip up, like he used to do when he was 'bout to ask a question, and he smiled.

"Let's do it again, Pansy," he said with delight and clapped his little hands.

"Not now," I said. "I'm goanna' let you swim in the big tub of water while I make it rain all over you!"

"Okay, Pansy," he shouted with glee, and he jumped up and down, almost fallin' backward down the stairs.

I pointed to the big room near the top of the stairs and the shiny white porcelain fixtures gleamed as much as his face did. "You go on in, Lil' Luke, and I'll fetch your nightshirt."

When I came back Lil' Luke was strugglin' with the buttons on his underwear.

"Let me get that for you, Lil' Luke," I said.

"I was busy helpin' Lil' Luke to undo the buttons on his underwear, and he was starin' out of the circular washroom window.

"Pansy," he asked. He pronounced it 'Pan Zee.' "Why is the sky blue?"

I was squeezin' my ears to hear what was goin' on downstairs while I sat unbuttonin' the buttons on Lil' Luke's undershirt. Lil' Luke had that special way of callin' my name that always broke through the cloud of thought constantly orbitin' my head. However annoyin' it was, I was always delighted to be with Lil' Luke and his steady stream of questions.

"Pansy, did you hear me? Why is the sky blue?"

"Now that is a mighty good question, Lil' Luke," I said.

I reckon he couldn't have asked me a better question since I had just had the lesson in my science class about stages of water in its forms of solid, liquid, and gas.

"If you squint your eyes you can see, there are little bubbles in the air, and they are so little you can't usually see them, but they're there just the same. Way out there in the open space, there are different gases, and when the light from the sun shines on the little bubbles after they have been surrounded by these other gases, the liquid inside the little bubbles gets heated up."

"Do you know what happens when the water in the tea kettle gets heated up?" I asked him.

"It starts to bounce up and down in the kettle, Pansy."

"That's right, and so does the water inside the little bubble," I struggled to explain. When we look up at the millions and millions of these little bubbles movin' so fast what we see is the white light comin' from the sun reflectin' the color blue. The heat from that 'ole sun keeps them bubbles movin' pretty fast," I continued while his eyes got wider and wider.

"Then, as the sun goes down, the bubbles move slower givin' off a darker color, until the sky is black. The black sky is what happens when the sun goes down and so does all the color that the white light reflected."

"What happens to the colors?" he asked.

"All the colors that the gases reflected get absorbed in the blackness. That's what makes the night sky black," I answered him with certainty—even though I knew plum well I had made half of that stuff up.

Lil' Luke jumped up and down in the tub of warm soapy water. For a minute, I thought he was pretendin' to be a gaseous bubble his self. I feel bad sometimes 'bout how dat boy neva' questioned a thing I said. He took it on faith, blind faith. I could'a tol' him da sky was green, he'd 'a believed me. It was wonderful havin' somebody look up to me like 'dat.'

I just looked at Lil' Luke and smiled. He had a special way of makin' me believe in myself. Sometimes, I know I wasn't completely scientific, but the interest he showed and the enthusiasm he had for learnin' made it more than worth the occasional stretch of 'da facts. I made sure he'd never be kept waitin', and I never turned down a question from him.

"Now thirty years done gone by and here you is askin' yo' ole Aunt Pansy some questions of your own, not too unlike yo' namesake."

"Great story, Aunt Pansy, but I really fail to see the connection."

"Oh, you'll see it. You may have to live another fifty years, but you'll see it."

"Yeah, but right now is when I need to see it. My skin is black. How many ways can I tell you? I am sold down the river before I even put a toe in the water. There's no real hope for winnin'."

"Boy, I'm tryin' to tell you somethin'. Don't you know when Mr. Washington came into Granville, there was no boys even finishin' eighth grade? You just can't see it yet, but you is the hope, livin', breathin', standin', and—against my better judgment, hee, hee—smokin,' too, just like the Outlaw men before you. They were the hope then, and you is the hope now."

"Hmm..." was all that Luke said.

"You wanna talk sold down the river? I wish you could try bein' a bull-headed and stubborn female in 1860 with a mind on nothin' else but education in a world that doesn't even believe in girls knowin' more than how to cook some buns or worse... get dey buns cooked."

"Aunt Pansy, I appreciate all this but..."

"But? But what? Ain't a single colored man alive today in 1942 got any hope seein' tomorrow, lessen' a few good black men lay their life on the line."

"What I'm saying, Aunt Pansy, with all due respect to you and the wonderful, really wonderful, tales about Pa and the good 'ole days, is that I have a noon train to catch and I'd better be getting along. But I do wonder if those stairs could talk, and they were the Alabama legislature, what they would say about a black man crossing that line."

"Boy, just remember one thin'. There wouldn't be no Alabama legislature if'n yo' daddy, under the direction of Mr. Washington's first Negro Army major, had not laid his very own life on that line."

"And because of him, I should be grateful that I don't have a daddy?" Luke shot back more harshly than he had intended. "I think maybe it would have been better if he had kept his yellow ass in Virginia!"

"Hold on right there, young man! It ain't fittin' to dishonor a hero, no matter what color he is. Eva'body goes to ashes, you know. There ain't a man livin', or dead for that matter, that I admire more than Mr. Washington."

"And I'm supposed to honor a man whose great plan for the Negro slave put my daddy in his grave?" Luke snapped.

"Why, Luke! Your father was a hero, too."

"My father was a free black educator and he had no business being sacrificed for some cowshit-slinging, shiftless, pig feet-sucking stogy."

"Luke!"

"Like I said, I've gotta' go."

And with that, Luke slammed shut the door to his past.

There was a time when I would have run him down and shook some sense into him like Mama Tutu often did to his pa. Even so, all I had the strength to do from my frail but stalwart body was to shake my finger at him furiously.

"That's the part that ain't black enough!" I screamed after his vanishin' back. "You'll hear more from me, young man, you just wait and see."

Chapter III

Sunday Morning, 1860

On Sundays when we didn't have a flock of the hungry sheep from church hangin' out on the front porch, I would be out prunin' and pinchin' dry leaves from my hangin' plants. Other times I planted seedlin's or sprouts I had rooted. Lil' Luke would always be close by. And all the while, Mama Tutu's melodious deep resonant voice echoed throughout the Judd mansion, often times with one of the 'ole spirituals. "Swing Low, Sweet Chariot" was what she was singin' right before she started lookin' for me.

"Where 'dat gal, Pansy? I'm 'bout finished pressin' huh dress. I bet she somewhere with her hands deep in dirt," she hollered, pausin' her singin'.

One time, I was outside growin' stuff from the seeds of stuff I had already grown—still busy pickin' and trimmin'—when suddenly I heard Lil' Luke hollerin' like it was the Fourth of July.

"Pansy! Pansy! Pansy!" he bellowed.

It was Huckabuck Marie. There she was, in clear view, struttin' down the road that winded right past the house. Even from the front you could see her behind. It shimmied from side to side and looked like a waterfall cascadin' over the rock solid bone and marrow of her shapely physique. She didn't just walk. She marched. She looked like an officer on a military mission, except she was dressed in fine silk taffeta with her skirt trailin' instead of a heavy dark wool uniform. I tried desperately not to look, yet I could see her undulatin' movements and the rustle of her ruffled buttress crept into the corner of my eye and the edge of my ears. I didn't know what to make of her. We hadn't become friends yet.

I could tell Huckabuck Marie was rushin' to another new job. She had a habit of walkin' straight without lookin' to the left or the right. In fact, she never looked at anyone. But you best believe no one ever missed her. Anybody caught within three feet of her in public would be relegated to hell, fire, and brimstone from the pulpit on Sunday mornin'. Condemnation of her crossed the lips of the faithful more times than the Lord's Prayer. It didn't bother her. She always kept right on walkin'. This time, she was goin' to the stagecoach junction for a trainin' class that Sunday and to pick up her new uniform. Her new job was goin' to be to collect the passes from the passengers as they boarded the coach. Later in the day, when she was on her way back, Lil' Luke didn't have any sense of restraint when he saw her. She was wearin' her new uniform and a necktie. It was the necktie that caught Lil' Luke's eyes.

"Pansy!" he screamed, "Look at them big titties under that tie. Who she think she foolin', she ain't no man."

"Hush up, Lil' Luke," I said, rebukin' my excited little brother.

It took all the self-control I could muster up not to look at Huckabuck Marie this time. That woman was sashayin' down the street proud as a peacock in her new uniform. Lil' Luke shook his little body from side to side creating a funny visual of her movements.

"Pansy, Pansy, look, it's Huckabuck, Huckabuck Marie, and she is prancin' down the street like a prize-winnin' mare."

"I told you to hush up, Lil' Luke," I sternly repeated.

"Oooo weee! Look at them muffins shake, rattle, and roll."

"Okay, that's enough, Lil' Luke. Can't you see the boards in this porch are loose and you're shakin' my plants?" I shouted.

At that moment a hand came out from behind the screen, snatched him up by the arm, and swung him around the door.

"What's all the commotion, boy?" chastised Mama Tutu. "You done loss your last mind."

She tickled me. She was famous for sayin' stuff like that. She always referred to the first mind as the one that got you into trouble.

"If you follow your first mind," she would say, "you 'goanna pay a big price, cause it ain't nothin' but trouble. Always wait for the second mind before you act. That's the one 'goanna steer you right." If your second mind didn't stop you from doin' somethin' stupid, then Mama Tutu would remind you that you had lost your "last mind" and then that's when she would take over for you.

Another thin' about Mama Tutu was that she could even cook a skunk and make it taste good. I never liked cookin' though. I heard my Mama from the porch remindin' Mama Tutu that there was only three more weeks until Mr. Washington was comin' to town.

"We should all make our favorite baked dish and have it ready to serve at Sunday dinner," Mama said as she rolled out the dough for her peach cobbler.

"I sho' like to see Pansy tryin' to do some cookin, at least for this special occasion," Mama Tutu responded. "But she is such a stubborn 'ole mule when it comes to 'dat kitchen."

It was true. My mama had tried to get me to practice bakin' for years. That was the first time I could remember showin' any interest in cookin' at all. I was so excited when I overheard them talkin' about the schoolmaster comin' that I rushed in to join the conversation, lettin' the door slam shut behind me.

"Where you think you are, gal, in a barn? You know betta' than to let that door slam like 'dat. If I was bakin' a cake, it would've fell right through the floor. Course what would you know about that? And what, may I ask, has you bustin' in here like a chargin' bull anyway? I know cookin' ain't never got you excited befo'."

"Please promise me, Mama Tutu, that you will not make a single cake without me?" I pleaded. I wanted to make a cake that Mr. Washington would never forget.

"Lawd a mercy! Somebody tell me dey heard Pansy say somethin' 'bout cookin'," Mama Tutu shouted.

Me, bakin'? Now that's a laugh. Back then, I'd stay as far away from the kitchen as I could. I betta' not go near that kitchen right now. Eva' time I goes in there. I seem to slip back in time. It starts to feelin' like all that stuff is hap-penin' all over again. Feels like I'm slippin' back and forth just sittin' at this table. Let me just take a little nap 'til Luke comes back.

Chapter IV

The Normal School

That nap took my mind on a back slide through time. I had much more in my memory than Luke had time to hear. Luke's anger reminded me of all the trouble I had dreamin' my dream. I had little hope. Can you imagine what it was like to have a mountain of hope while standin' in a valley of quicksand? Was it even possible to be a female scientist in 1860? I had my nerve, or so everyone said.

The future certainly did not come alive for me in the kitchen, that's for sure. Everythin' in there had already been killed and was waitin' to be cooked. The only thin' alive was the burnin' ember that was thrown under the skillet to keep it burnin'. That big black skillet made me think of greedy ole' Pritchard Kemp lyin' on top of some sizzlin' hot virgin, snuffin' out any chance her flame may have to ignite and lighten any other life but his. He always made us girls feel like property. No suh, I decided long ago that I would not sacrifice a moment of my future on any of those dusty church deacons with dey potbellies and bad breath. I never shined in the kitchen no how. Now school that was where I lit up, and I mean lit up like a firecracker.

After Luke left the house, I could feel myself slippin' into one of those far away naps, the ones that take me back to my youth. Before I knew it, there I was back at the farm school where my dream was born.

At twelve years old, I was already in my eighth year of schoolin'. One day when I was rummagin' through my desk after school had let out, I overheard two of my teachers talkin' about the new Normal School. I was doin' my regular day-dreamin' my childhood dream about makin' an unforgettable impact on the conscience of the rural South. I was sittin' there in front of the desk just pretendin' that it was a lectern and I was givin' a speech in a town where most girls didn't finish dey primary grades.

"This here potato will grow bigger and better when you add a little ash to the soil to help give more oxygen to the roots," I'd imagine myself sayin' to a crowd of farmers attendin' an outdoor science fair. I believed I would change the course of history as a Negro educator and my contribution to science would also radically change the attitudes toward women in the South. Deep in my sleep now, I could hear my teachers talkin', and I was magically taken right back there again.

"Did you know he intends to sell his bricks to white men from the north?" said Jasper Ale, standin' stiff like a crane with one leg propped on a chair. He didn't really believe in educatin' folk about labor and trade.

"You eva' seen a brick bein' sold at the flea market?" he asked.

"I ain't. There's no sense in makin' white men rich off of your invention anyhow. What kind of fool is this fella?" Mr. Pritchard Kemp asked. Now Mr. Pritchard was the worst teacher in the whole schoolhouse. He hardly ever moved from standin' behind his desk. I think he used it to hold his stomach up. This was really disgustin' since he had sloppily piled all the student permission slips for the Normal School right next to his sweaty ole belly.

"You got me, Kemp. He already had been workin' with dem savage injuns in Virginia 'bout how to grow more crops. He tellin' folks that the way crops grow better is by what you put in de dirt. I heard he saw dem injuns mixin' crap from da farm animals and puttin' it in de ground where de seeds are bein' planted," Jasper Ale said.

"Now he got injuns makin' bricks. Dey says word of da sales done got all da way up to Delaware," he continued. "You know how dem injuns is, befo' you can saddle up a pony dey news done traveled cross-country and you be hearin' talk of de reaction to da news back home. And from what I heard, dem injuns is already doublin' dey's yield. Can you believe, in spite of eva'tin' he done for dem, I don't see one of dem flat foots offerin' to put n'ere one brick on da new school that Mr. Washington is down here tryin' to build. Do you think for one minute dey cares 'bout you and me?" Jasper Ale continued his rantings. "Well, I'll tell you," he added. "Dey only cares about dey own."

"Den, why do you s'pose Mr. Washington is spendin' all his time wit dem injuns anyhow?" Mr. Pritchard Kemp probed.

"Cause da Negroes up in Virginia don't care nothin' 'bout no farmin'," Jasper Ale answered. "I s'pect that's why he's comin' down here because he needs our farm boys to open up dis Normal School," he continued, gesturin' toward the open fields.

"He must be thinkin' wez brawny Negroes down here in Alabama. 'Cause we ain't tryin' too hard to learn from dem books," continued Mr. Kemp.

"Mosta' our boys is happy to be workin' and some of dem is still on dey 'ole plantations while da others is in the fields where dey think dey belongs. You know how long I been tryin' to get dem out of da fields? What we need is someone to teach them how to read and write. Use their brain more than dey back."

"Mr. Washington is smart 'nough to know wez farmin' folks," Jasper Ale continued.

"Matta' fact, when I spoke wif him 'bout da arrangements for his hospitality at Ole' Man Judd's house, he was spectin' to sleep in da barn!"

The two men burst out in laughter.

"Haaaahh! Haaaahh!" Jasper Ale went on, still gigglin', "Can't 'magine no Southern Negroes wit mo' than one-room houses. I reckon he gonna git a little schoolin' his self.

"How many eighth-grade boys you got, Kemp?" Jasper Ale asked.

"The last eighth-grade boy we had in 'dis here schoolhouse just dropped out April past," Pritchard Kemp replied.

"See what I mean!" Jasper Ale shouted. "Our boys ain't tryin' to fill up dey minds with a whole lot of stuff what don't have nothin' to do with dem. Dey's practical farmin' boys. Dey knows dey gotta work. Dey know how to do da work and dey know what work is fo' dem and dey know dat dat work is in de field. Mr. Washington believes in learnin' deese here boys how to do da field work betta'. But does he understand dat deese is field boys? I'll tell you what he thinkin', Kemp, and he tol' me dis his self. He said, 'If deese boys don't be stayin' in de schoolhouse, wez jus' gonna have to take da schoolhouse out to dem in de fields.' I had a mind to tell him wez been schoolin' boys befo' he knew his butt from a groundhog's hole in the ground."

Of course dey was payin' no attention to me. It was like I wasn't even in the room. I heard dem talkin' about learnin' out in the fields and I was beside myself with excitement. I continued to fumble through the box lookin' for the letter from Mama givin' me permission to apply to the Normal School. I nearly dropped the whole stack of papers from my hand when I heard Mr. Kemp say that Mr. Washington knew how to cultivate seeds and to fertilize soil with a mixture of minerals and sand. I too was good with soil. All those days in the barn makin' firewood out of cow dung and hay and smellin' its rotten stench bakin' in the hot sun was finally gonna pay off. I loved to mix things, I was thinkin'. Shucks, I already had my very own brand of cleansin' soap, which I made from all the scraps around the shed. I collected those scraps for months in a big glass jug until I had enough to melt down and make bars of soap. Sometimes I added dried flowers to give it a sweet smell, so it wasn't like the tar smellin' soap that Mama used to wash clothes. My head was spinnin' with desire, and then finally I found the letter.

"I'm gonna be an inventor, too," I interrupted, holdin' up the letter.

"We know you is," said Mr. Kemp. "You is gonna invent a slew of little smart rascals just like yo'se'f and dey's gonna take up every seat in this here 'ole schoolhouse," he chuckled.

"Yes suh, I believe Little Missy Outlaw is gonna double her mama's production line. By the way," asked Mr. Jasper Ale, "Wasn't I noticin' you and Joshua whisperin' at each other cross that aisle 'fo ya'll lef' out a here last week?"

"Why, yes, Mr. Jasper, but we was tryin' to figure out how we was gonna pay for our education at the Normal School when it opened," I said timidly. Both men broke out in loud boisterous laughter, slappin' their sides.

Mr. Jasper Ale, pointin' his finger from side to side like a metronome, "Uh ah, oh no," he said. "Ain't no gals gonna to be goin' to da new school."

I was devastated. My heart sank like a rock down a well. It was clear as a church bell that I could not depend on the support of my teachers. I folded my permission letter and tucked it in my sweater pocket and headed for the door mumblin' curses under my breath about rat tails and devil horns.

"I am too, you'll see, and I don't need ya'll to tell me if I can" I yelled back over my shoulder. "I don't need nobody. Nobody, you hear! Nobody, 'cept my Mama Tutu!"

I bolted out of the schoolhouse lettin' the screened door slam and kept running. All of a sudden, my dream was danglin' like an old broken screen on its hinges. Didn't I win the blue ribbon at the science fair? Didn't I come in first at the hometown spellin' bee? And didn't my math scores top every student in the eighth grade, girl or boy? Ain't I the one supposed to go to the Normal School? If not, who is? Jasper Ale, of all people, knew I was supposed to go. Why does he hate me so? What on earth is this talk about gals not goin'? My thoughts were racin' through my mind and my body just took off!

I ran across the field to the dirt road where Josh and I had walked every day to school together. Most boys didn't quite make it to the last year in Mr. Kemp's schoolhouse. By the time they can carry a bale of hay or can drive some horses, they are used in the fields on the family plot whilst the older men went out to do the sharecrop work on neighboring plantations. Not much reason for a Negro to know about things contained in books, unless his mama or papa was a teacher. Most of them planned to live by the sweat of their brow, not things dey gonna learn from books.

I kept runnin' until I reached my secret spot, and then I scurried up to the top of my treehouse. When I stopped, I realized that my sweater was hangin' from the ends of my wrists and the sweat was pourin' from my brow. I wiped my sleeve across my forehead, and then I pulled it the rest of the way off and threw it into a far corner of my hide-a-way shelter. I pulled out one of the books I had stacked along the walls and started writin' in it furiously.

I could feel the pencil cuttin' into the paper as I wrote: "I ain't gonna be no slave. I ain't gonna pick no cotton. I ain't gonna have a heap of nappy headed children and I ain't gonna let nobody tell me what I'm gonna do. Signed, Pansy Outlaw, May 23, 1859."

"Pansy!" I could hear my name wrappin' itself around the house that I shared with Grandma Tutu, Mama, Papa, and my baby brother, Lil' Luke. I sat still for a minute before decidin' to answer the call. I didn't think anyone had seen whether or not I was home from school. Sometimes my mama knows things, and I can't imagine how she knows them.

I started down the tree. Still, I wasn't settled down, so I went back up to my little hide-a-way, which I believed was the safest place in the whole mean world. I thought of all the changes I had seen in my twelve short years of life. I knew that one day I would outgrow the place that held so many memories for me. Most of them I kept in that hidden diary. I was truly missin' Josh that day. Usually he would listen to my problems up there in that treehouse.

My diary preserves the story about the mornin' that he first arrived. It was the day when Josh first moved to town with his mama and two sisters. If a peanut had legs and a head it would'a been 'bout as big as him. It makes me chuckle thinkin' of the first time I saw Josh. He was hidin' under the porch and all I could see was the whites of his eyes, his eyeballs rollin' back with fear. Our family dog, Bingo, had tried to lick the fat back off the top of his head. It was me who helped him. That big ole dog towered over Josh, and by placin' one paw on each shoulder, he knocked Josh over and did a belly flop on top of him. Before I even knew what had happened, chickens were squawkin' and runnin' in all directions and Josh was way up under the middle of the house. I laughed all night over that, and that was the beginnin' of many days of laughter with Josh after his mama and two sisters moved in with us, takin' refuge from her bad marriage.

It took him a couple of years to get over his fear of dogs after that, but he did, and him and Bingo got to be real good friends. You couldn't see Josh without seein' Bingo. Bingo even slept in the same bed with Josh.

"As long as that animal sleeps anywhere near that bed, you'll never catch me in it," proclaimed Josh's older sister. "No, not ever," she repeated on numerous occasions. She would rather sleep at the foot of her mama's bed than to share the big guest room with Josh and Bingo.

"A dog is a man's best friend," Josh would always say when she asked him to make Bingo sleep in the yard. "So what you're askin' me is to kick my friend out?" he'd ask with a big grin.

"That's not fair," she screamed. "We sleepin' three in one, and he's got one all to himself."

"You're welcome to come any time," he'd answer.

"Ugh, please! I'd rather sleep on nails," his sister replied.

"Me, too," added his younger sister.

So Josh and Bingo were partners for everythin'. Everywhere Josh went, Bingo would follow. Sometimes they went fishin' and Bingo would carry the basket of tackle tied around his neck. At dinner time, I could see Josh slippin' table scraps under the tablecloth, and Bingo would not move from Josh's side even when others would drop a treat or two. I loved Bingo, too, but not like Josh did. It was hard to believe how much he became attached to him. That first attack would'a scared most children off for good. I reckon that dog was somethin' like a father to Josh. Sort of made up for the father he didn't have. He wouldn't let a soul get near Josh. His own mama was afraid to scold him 'cause Bingo would let out a growl muffled behind his full set of clenched canine teeth. It was a real shame when that dog had to go. Josh pleaded with Papa not to put him down, but he had to do it.

I knew Bingo was sick 'cause Josh asked me to get some of the horse vitamins from the barn and mix it in his food, which I did. That gave him a little more energy for a while 'til he stopped eatin' altogether. It was bad. Whatever he had, it was eatin' him up from inside. The skin on his body looked like a wet rug hangin' on a tree branch. Papa held off until Josh was ready and they took him out to the barn early one Sunday mornin' where Papa put him out of his misery.

First, I heard the shot and then I heard Josh sobbin'. Papa said Josh held Bingo in his arms with the blood-stained blanket wrapped around his head until he stopped breathin'. Then Josh carried Bingo to the grave Papa had prepared behind the barn and laid his friend to rest. Papa let Josh cover the grave over and Josh placed a pair of sticks tied in a cross on top of the mound of dirt.

After that Papa told Josh about a litter of pups that he knew about in town.

"I reckon I could offer you for work in exchange for one of those new puppies I heard was born the other day," Papa said to Josh.

"I'm afraid not," Josh replied. "Whenever I start to lovin' somethin' real good, it don't stay around."

"Why you sayin' that, Josh?" I asked. "I love you more than I love anyone, well, maybe 'cept for Papa, oh, and Mama Tutu."

"See that don't mean nothin'," Josh quickly replied. "Already I'm last on the totem pole. You just tryin' to make me feel good."

"Am not," I said.

"Are so," he replied.

It wasn't too long after that day, one of the churchwomen decided that Josh and I was too old to be livin' in the same house. They wanted to send him to another home to live with one of the deacons who had a barren wife.

I begged Papa not to let them take Josh away. I told Papa, "Josh ain't never did nothin' wrong." He knew that, too, but he still let them talk him into givin' Josh to another family.

I missed Josh, and after he left, I had nowhere to turn to for solace except for my treehouse and in the lovin' arms of Mama Tutu. In both places I could escape from the cripplin' small minds of Granville's pompous social scavengers.

Yet even there, I heard my mama's shrill voice echo in the empty wooden box where I sat perched between the limbs.

"Pansy, you hear me callin' you, girl!" she yelled, breakin' the silence of my thoughts. "If I have to come after you, you gonna be fetchin' a switch!"

That was enough of a warnin' for me. I took the fast way—slidin' down the trunk of the 'ole hide-a-way—and yelled out loud and clear, "I'm comin', Mama!" as I raced toward the back door and jumped over the septic tank on my way to the kitchen. I sprinted toward the porch to leap up the two steps like I usually did, and I was struck by a cluster of violet wild flowers peerin' through the gap in the stairs. I stopped, nearly in mid-flight, and swung around the railin' to pick a bunch for the dinner table. I was on my knees gatherin' the flowers when I noticed clusters of three-leaf clovers scattered about the rugged little natural sanctuary. I rubbed my hand reverently across their faces and whispered greetin's to each and every one of them. Out of the corner of my eye, I spotted what looked like a clover with four leaves. When I scooted under the stairs to get a closer look and pushed away the other clovers sur-roundin' it, there it was. Flashin' before my eyes, as dazzlin' as a silver dollar in the hands of a beggar, was a four-leaf clover. I carefully pulled it from the soft spring earth and held it gently to my lips. This is my lucky day, I thought, and I turned to gather the wild flowers. I walked into the kitchen proudly bearin' a floral gift bouquet and presented them to Mama.

"Here, Mama, this is for the table."

"And I suppose that is your way of makin' up for not settin' the table," she replied.

"Oh, no, Mama, I brought those to make the table pretty. The reason I'm late is I was writin' in my journal, and I got to thinkin' about the times when Josh was here."

"How about thinkin' about the present times a little more and remem-berin' to be on time for your chores so I won't have to do them for you."

"Yes, ma'am," I promised sheepishly.

Mama was my first teacher. Nobody knew how she learned how to read. The story goes that when Mama Tutu heard she was courtin' Papa, she sent her over to France just to get her trained in how to be high society. Over there she had a tutor who taught her about classic English books. When she returned to Granville she was better educated than the whole grammar school staff. She also knew all the social graces about entertainin', which was most likely why she organized all the church socials, with Mama Tutu's help of course. The Outlaw mansion was the main location of many church and social events.

Although my mama was a good housekeeper, she did not care for house chores the way some of the other townswomen seemed to care. She believed her hands were too delicate for heavy soaps and scourin'. So that's how she lived as though cleanin' "was someone else's" job. Mama Tutu used to say she was sorry she ever sent my mama to France because that "someone else" usually ended up bein' her, doin' all the housework.

"We ain't descendants of slaves, you know, Pansy," Mama said. "Not that I have anythin' at 'tall against n'ere one of them, I just can't be bothered with them and their ways. They know housework like puppies know rootin' for tits. Not me, nor da ancestors. We were free blacks who migrated from the West Indies. We was civilized befo' we even came to the South. Did you know our ancestors escaped from dem slave tradin' vessels?" she asked. "We owned a sugar cane plantation which 'till this day is why Mama Tutu thinks I have dirt under my finger nails," Mama said as she continued makin' iced tea. "These hands ain't never touched the dirt. I let her think what she wants though 'cause she would kill me if she ever knew that we had slaves," Mama whispered.

I wanted to know more about that and, since Mama was busy with dinner, I knew not to ask about it then. I started thinkin', if our ancestors escaped slave ships, I knew I could make it to the Normal School. Later that night when my mama was strugglin' to braid my hair befo' bedtime, I asked her all about it, and then I asked her about my application.

"Mama, am I goin' to be the only girl applyin' for the Normal School?"

"That ain't nothin' to start to worryin' 'bout, gal, since you is jus' as good as any boy in town when it comes to your schoolin'. Now finish gettin' yo'sef ready for bed. A chile that's rested is a chile that's ready! Tomorrow, I know you gonna' be ready to show fat ole Mr. Kemp that the Outlaws ain't raisin' no sloth."

I smiled and ran up the stairs. A tepid bath was waitin' for me and Mama Tutu was sittin' by the tub.

Chapter V

Mama Tutu's Care

Without Mama Tutu, baths were unbearable. She was always able to ease my burdens. Mama Tutu not only made things feel better, she made them fun. She would make sure that all the important parts got cleaned and would always cuddle me up on her big soft lap after she had dried me off and buttoned up all the buttons on my long johns, same as I did for Lil' Luke. My mama hated that I liked long johns instead of a nightdress, but Mama Tutu didn't mind. I really believed I had long outgrown that ritual, but as long as Mama Tutu would continue to do it, I would continue to have it done.

It seemed I was at war with the whole world some days, and her tender nurturin' was a release of all stress, like meltin' butter on hot cakes, so soothin' to my soul. I especially liked it when she would sing my favorite song. And of all her sweet and soulful lullabies, the one she created for me was the best. It echoes through my mind as clear as crystal. She must be singin' it in paradise.

"Oh my baby, my little baby. Oh my dahlin', sweet little girl. Sweet little, sweet little, sweet little girl. Strong and smarter than any in the world," she sang on a many occasion, to my delight. It was how my day ended. Whenever she sang that song, there was no mountain that appeared insurmountable. Whenever there was somethin' in my day that seemed impossible, it was that song that sounded the victory. From her lap, all things were possible.

Mama Tutu said she had somethin' special for me in preparation for the upcomin' holiday. Independence Day was always a huge celebration in Granville, but the one that summer was magnificent. The first-generation freed slaves could not contain themselves. It was a time when everyone put on their best clothes and lined the main street to watch the parade pass. People went to be seen more than to see, so it was Mama Tutu's idea to give me a hair treatment in anticipation of the event. It was a long process and I can remember the fight I put up.

"Hold still, girl, I'm almost done. This creams 'gonna take all the naps outta yo' hair. You gonna look so pretty, why, Mr. Washington gonna want to get rid of whatever women he wit, once he sees you. Next thin' you know he be askin' yo' Papa fo' yo' hand in marriage. No matta' that you's a baby girl, he gonna' want to grab you now fo' da future."

"Like he'll even notice some scrawny little black girl," I said.

"Ooooooooo wee, look at 'ya," she squealed. "You might not be yella' lack him, but yo hair is as straight and shiny as da queen of England. Okay, you can open yo' eyes now," Mama Tutu directed.

She shouted and hollered like she used to do when she was gettin' the Holy Spirit. She held the silver rimmed mirror in front of my face, but I was scared to open my eyes. I squinted a tiny bit open and then shut them tight. This went on for a while.

"Girl, what is wrong with you? I said open yo' eyes, not shut them tighter. You ain't got nothin' to be so scared fo'," she said, urgin' me to look in the mirror.

I reached up to the top of my head to feel my hair.

"Ahhhhhhhhhh! Where's my hair?" I screamed.

"Girl, yo' hair is still on yo' head. You just ain't used to feelin' it flat down against yo' scalp," she said, tryin' to reassure me.

I felt very slowly down toward my ear and touched the side of my head.

"Oh God, you done burned all my hair out!" I yelled.

"Girl, you need to get hold of yo'sef and open dem eyes. Come on, chile, see fo' yo'sef. You got hair and you got a long and beautiful braid hangin' down pass yo' shoulders," she said.

Mama Tutu just stood in front of me holdin' out the mirror by its delicately ornate stem. "Now you know yo' Mama Tutu not gonna' let anything bad happen to you or no part of you," she said, attemptin' to reassure me. "Whatcha' waitin' fo'? Christmas done passed and my arms bout to stiffin' up from holdin' up dis heah mirror," she complained.

She stood in front of me tall and straight with the stature of a giant owl. She wasn't really tall. She just looked tall.

"You promise me my hair is there?" I pleaded.

"I promise," replied Mama Tutu.

I slowly re-opened my eyes without squeezin' them back shut 'til they got halfway opened. As I focused clearly, what I saw was amazin'. I had silky smooth lines of shiny black hair brushed back into a long braid. My mouth fell wide open. In successively higher pitches you could hear my voice through the whole house. "Ahhh, aahhh, aaahhh," I bellowed higher and higher.

"You see, chile, you can trust Mama Tutu. I got this stuff straight from the sac of Madame B. Wells. I saw her sales tent on Main Street the other day and she got it straight off the ship from Germany at 'da port in Mobile. You'll be the first one wit' it in all of Granville."

The day after was Sunday, and my Lord, there was so much hootin' and hollerin' after church about my new hairstyle. Folks kept makin' me turn around and show off. The churchwomen made such a fuss and Mama Tutu was explainin' to eva'body about the new product. I felt like a china doll sittin' in the window. By nighttime I was startin' to get used to it, but I knew I would never survive the ridicule at the schoolhouse. The followin' day was proof.

When I arrived in front of the old school house, my cousin Joshua was comin' up the road.

"Pansy, is that you?" he yelled from the road.

"Yeah it's me Josh, and don't you say nothin'."

"Don't say nothin' about what, Pansy?"

As soon as he got close enough to see, his jaw dropped. "What the heck?"

"Hush up, Josh, I'm warnin' you." I raised my fist and twisted my mouth, the way I did when I was about to hall off and hit somebody.

"Okay, okay, I'm not sayin' nothin', but how you gonna' 'splain that to Mr. Kemp? He ain't gonna know who you are and when he find out it's you, you in big trouble."

"Trouble for what? I ain't done nothin'."

"Umph, he'll find somethin'. He's been buggin' eva' since you started that stuff about goin' to the Normal School. You know how the men in this town feel about educatin' gals. Only reason you still in this here school is 'cause yo' mama don't need you in the fields. Anybody else would be pickin' cotton by now. Just be careful, Pansy. Don't give him any reason to notice you and sit low in your chair so that big Hunt boy will block you from his view. Oh and here, wear this hat."

But as soon as I walked into the classroom, Mr. Kemp stopped me at the door.

"Just a minute, young lady, I believe you owe me an apology for slammin' this classroom door yesterday. Don't think you can be in so much of a hurry that you can't take the time to be polite in this school."

"Yes, sir. Sorry, sir," I said, tryin' desperately to get to my seat.

"Hold it, hold it, little lady. Where do you think you are goin' with that hat on your head?"

I froze and looked sideways at Josh, out of the corner of my eye. Josh kept on walkin' and slipped halfway onto the seat behind his desk. He lifted up his desktop and peeped around it to see. His desk tilted, he grabbed the top, and the whole desk fell.

"What's the matter with you? Are you drunk, boy?" screamed Mr. Kemp.

"No, sir, it was an accident sir. Sorry, sir," replied Josh, tryin' to push the desk off of him.

Everybody burst out laughin'. 'Course all the while he was tryin' to distract Mr. Kemp from my hair and me. He then managed to push the desk with his foot and sent it crashin' into the desk next to his.

"Can you please get yourself under control, Mr. Talliafaro," insisted Mr. Kemp.

At this point I was easin' down the aisle toward my desk, which was next to Josh's desk on the other side.

"Excuse me, Ms. Outlaw, but where do you think you are goin'?"

"I was goin' to sit down, sir."

"You're not goin' anywhere in this classroom with a hat on your head. Return to the front of the class immediately." Mr. Kemp had a way of drivin' a point into the ground. Everythin' was an example to him. He took every opportunity to humiliate any student for even the smallest transgression, just so he could use them to keep the rest of the class under control. Josh and/or I were often the ones chosen for this position of dishonor. Today was a particularly sensitive time for it to be me.

"Before you go anywhere, remove that hat, young lady," he said harshly.

"I can't, Mr. Kemp," I said.

"And why, may I ask, can't you?" he asked.

"Well, because...well, you see... " I could not think of one good reason why I couldn't take off the hat so I simply reached up and slid it down past my shoulder and dropped my hand by my side, clutchin' it.

"Well, look a here. Ain't enough to be the po'est lookin' little rich gal in Granville, but now I reckon you gonna' tell me you been scalped by some injuns." Mr. Kemp slowly approached me and noticed that I still had hair but it was slicked down close to my head. "Oh, this is fun," he said and grabbed the long braid hangin' down my back. "Look at this," he jeered, holdin' the braid up. "Maybe you is an injun yo'self."

The whole class, except for Josh, burst into laughter again. I snatched my head to the side and Mr. Kemp dropped the braid.

"Temper, temper, Miss Pansy Outlaw, I don't intend to be disrespected by you again today, you know. Now tell me, how many injuns you hidin' up in that 'ole mansion?"

I was so angry that the tears began to well up in my eyes. I didn't know anyone could be so cruel.

"May I sit down now, Mr. Kemp?" I asked.

"Not until you do us a rain dance." He turned to the class. "We need some rain round deez parts, don't we, ya'll?

"Yes, sir, Mr. Kemp," the class chimed.

"Well, class, here stands injun Pansy Outlaw, miss don't-wanna-be-rich but wanna-be-smart gal, who's gonna do us a rain dance."

At this point Josh jumped up from his seat and said, "That's enough."

Mr. Kemp twirled around on his heels and, addressin' the class, said, "My fellow students, it is quite evident that Mr. Talliafaro and Miss Outlaw are both from the same tribe. Maybe it is now time to give them a lesson in civilization.

"I know you ain't spectin' me to write a letter to the Normal School for no injun when wez got black boys who is just as smart and know how to follow directions. You either do the rain dance or get a floggin' for disobedience," he warned.

"Fetch me the paddle, young man."

He pointed to the nearest student who jumped up and got the paddle out from under Mr. Kemp's desk.

"I said, that's enough!" Josh yelled this time.

Now, Josh was no tough boy, but he was big. When he saw Mr. Kemp takin' the paddle to my rear end, he stormed down the aisle toward him.

Mr. Kemp raised that rough oak paddle and said, "Civilized people follow directions or they get whipped."

Before the paddle came down, Josh grabbed Mr. Kemp by the forearm and came up from below his chin with the full force of his right fist.

"Huhhhhh," shouted the whole class in chorus.

Mr. Kemp went stumblin' backward against the chalkboard and slid down to the floor. He was out. I ran out of the class, down the hall, and swished pass Mr. Jasper Ale's storeroom office. I kept runnin' until I got home; Joshua wasn't far behind me. Mama Tutu was sweepin' the porch and saw me runnin' up the road. Then Josh bursts through the cloud of dust that followed behind me. We were runnin' like hell was behind us. Mama Tutu was waitin', her arms open wide. She could see the anguish in my face.

"Whatever it is, chile, it's gonna be all right, baby. It's gonna be all right."

I fell into her warm embrace and she patted my back with her strong wide palm. Josh stood by watchin'.

I cried and tried to explain what had just happened, but I couldn't speak clearly through the sobbin'. The strength of Mama Tutu's muscular arms around me made me feel safe. Her arms were strong, like arms grown taut from pickin' bales of cotton and carryin' them across miles of plantations in the South, yet she had never touched a cotton harvest. All she ever toted was water from the well and babies through the 'ole Judd mansion. It was those arms that gave me such comfort.

"There's no hope; I'll never get in the Normal School now," I cried. "Josh and me got in so much trouble at school," I continued. "And it is all because of this stupid new hairdo. I'm ruined. Mr. Kemp will never see me as a scholar, so I might as well just quit school altogether," I said, as Josh just stood there hemmin' and hawin' and scratchin' his head.

"You don't have to quit just 'cause somebody else don't see what you see. You just keep your eye on the prize, baby girl," Mama Tutu replied. "My little baby gonna be somebody big, and the day will come when all them phonies who was scared to change gonna be askin' for yo' 'pinion for they is able to say anythin'," boasted Mama Tutu.

I continued sobbin' 'til I couldn't see through the streams of tears wellin' up in my eyes. I cried and cried until Josh started to try to explain.

"You know how they don't lak to see gals be smarter than the men 'round here? Pansy, well, she know more about stuff than anybody in the class," he said.

"And I just know they ain't gonna let me in de new school 'cause I ain't no man. Mr. Kemp even says he wouldn't write me a letter even if I were a man 'cause now I look like an injun!" I begin sobbin' bitterly.

"Since when what de say eva' stopped da women in dis family?" Mama Tutu yelled so it shocked me right out of my grief. "If we got to dress you like a man, den send you there, we'll do just that," she continued defiantly. "But I do declare, when Mr. Washington gets the letter Reverend Smith is sendin' from Faith United, makin' reference to some little girl I know, it won't matter if you is a man, women, injun, or cow poke, you'll show that blunderin' idiot who's who."

"Oh, Mama Tutu," I asked through my tears, "what are you sayin'?"

"What I'm sayin', sweet-thing, is either you is gonna' be 'cepted in that school or Mr. Washington will have to find another town to build it in."

Mama Tutu let out a hearty, belly-rollin' laugh, and for the first time, I truly believed I would have the chance I had been waitin' for. I smothered my face in her bosom and filled her apron with tears. Those tears of sorrow that now turned into tears of joy. Mama Tutu began to rock me gently as she sang a very familiar song to me.

"Oh my baby, my little baby. Oh my dahlin' sweet little girl. Sweet little, sweet little, sweet little girl. Strong and smarter than any in the world."

"You're just the greatest, Mama Tutu, you are just the greatest," I sighed, lookin' up to her with my soakin' wet, big, happy, bet-I-can-do-it, brown, grateful eyes.

"She's the greatest, ain't she, Josh?" I said.

Josh nodded in agreement. "I reckon she must know somin'," he said.

Josh was right. She knew a whole lot of somin'.

Chapter VI

Three Weeks Later

"Don't nobody have nothin' to do but stand 'round in front of dis house, actin' lack deys waitin' for Jesus. Ain't nobody read de word where it says he comin' like a thief in the night. So go on, ya'll, get. We'll send for you when he comes." Mama Tutu stood in the doorway wavin' her arms like she was shooin' hogs.

"Pansy, you come on in here. Ain't you got some chores to finish?"

"I'm all done!" I replied with excitement.

"You all done, what?" she corrected.

"I'm all done, ma'am," I answered properly.

"Humph. I know you smart, chile, but I hope you ain't too smart to re-member your manners."

"No, ma'am!" I quickly replied.

"'Cause I 'spose you want some teeth behind that wide grin's gonna be plastered all over your face when he get here. I reckon when da Lawd do come, he gonna wish his name was Mr. Washington, way ya'll is waitin' and starin'," Mama Tutu said, laughin'.

"Oh, now hold on, Mama T," Jasper Ale interrupted, "I ain't seen you sit down since church this mornin'."

"Wasn't that you standin' up most of da time dere, testifyin' 'bout Mr. Washington and his school? Why to hear you talkin', we ain't had a teachin' man here since the slave boat dropped the English professor off in Mobile wit dem Negroes from Africa."

Jasper Ale got to preachin' and there was no tellin' when he would stop.

"Heh! Heh! I saw an article in the Harper's Weekly Journal said it took the professor damn near a whole year 'fo they found their way up the road and wandered into Granville," snickered Jasper Ale, the schoolmaster.

"Must notta' been too smart," responded young Pritchard Kemp. (He was the teacher I didn't have much liken' for, from the Granville farm school.) "The trip should only take five hours max," he sneered.

Everybody burst out laughin', cept me.

Pritchard Kemp continued, "Had a little trouble with the injuns, I reckon. Them injuns can sho' slow down a trip. Lucky for Mr. Washington, he done learned how to talk some of that injun talk, so he ain't got to worry none about no ambush from them."

"Lessen' he ridin' a stagecoach," added young Joshua. "Shoot, ain't a stage coach movin'—anywhere, from here to Virginia and back—that don't get stopped by them injuns," Josh said, like he was a travelin' man himself.

While all the men were cuttin' up and tellin' their native stories, a huge stallion, shinin' like freshly tanned black leather, had quietly stopped in front of the horse trowel to get a drink. The horse's coat was shimmerin' from the sweat pourin' down his neck. The man sittin' in the saddle was leanin' back so he looked twice as tall as the horse. He raised his hat from his head and wiped his brow with his forearm. From where I was standin', with the sun behind him, I could see his brawny skin givin' off tints of copper from his reddish hair. When he almost dropped his wide brim buckskin hat, I jumped. He caught it before it fell to the ground and, with a swift rhythmic circular hand movement, he saluted the sky with it. He looked as though he were payin' tribute to a great white cloud that floated overhead and created a silver linin'. I was immediately in awe of him.

I was the first to see him. I knew all the Indian attack stories by heart, which is why I wasn't payin' much attention to the others. When I looked toward the waterin' trowel, it was as if I saw Moses walkin' across the Red Sea. Then the sun slid from behind the cloud and, clear as day, it was the awesome figure of a man destined to alter the course of my life. He tugged the reins of his horse and gently guided it toward the rail right in front of the porch. Then he stopped and tipped his buckskin hat again and bowed his head toward Mama Tutu. By then she was frantically untyin' the apron from around her waist, flippin' it over her shoulder and landin' it on one of the hooks stickin' out from the Oakwood dressin' mirror on the wall in the foyer. I stood up from the wicker porch chair like I was movin' through honey, never once takin' my fixed stare off the eyes of my travel-weary savior. It was one of my rare but noticeably speechless moments; Jasper Ale realized by the look on my face that the schoolmaster had arrived.

Jasper Ale turned from all the neighbors and friends to greet Mr. Washington in typical Granville style, "Well, howdah do, stranger? Why don't ya fall in and stay a little while?"

"Why, thank you, brother, I don't mind if I do," Mr. Washington responded, instantly winnin' the affection of 'ole Jasper Ale, the town historian.

"A man who calls me brother," Jasper Ale replied, "don't ever have to worry where he's gonna lay his head at night."

"You have no idea how much that means to me," Mr. Washington said, as he dismounted the huge black stallion.

Right away Jasper Ale took over the introductions and introduced Mr. Washington to all the men gathered. I kept clearin' my throat but it wasn't until I had done it three or four times that he finally paid attention to me. By then, I was standin' in the dirt road right in front of Mr. Washington, shiftin' back and forth. Jasper Ale, finally noticin' me, and realizin' he had thoughtlessly left me out, made a wide gesture fannin' his hat through the air and bowin' as he introduced me.

"Miss Pansy Outlaw, sir."

I extended my hand and curtseyed. "My honor, Mr. Washington," I said.

"And may I present the matron of the house, Madame Tutu."

"Go on Jasper Ale, I don't need no introduction," she said in a bellowin' pitch.

Mama Tutu was runnin' down the porch steps, clackin' her cloth slippers loud against the wood, with her arms wide open and face beamin'. She rushed toward him and did a quick curtsey, mostly for the benefit of the crowd gathered. Next thing you know, she was jumping up and down all over his Wellingtons until she had him in a huge embrace.

"It's been too long, Mr. Washington," she said as they danced a circle in the dust, arms locked around each other's waist.

"It's been too too long," she said over again.

That evenin' dinner was at the church family hall. By the time we finished dinner, the display of cakes and pies was so elaborate that I was relieved knowin' that probably Mr. Washington would never know one cherry pie from another. I was sittin' with the guests at the guest table in a chair right next to the guest of honor, and I made sure not to mention the desserts. I was afraid that Mr. Washington might ask me which of them I had made. My biggest fear wasn't that he wouldn't like my bakin' but that he may have asked me how I made it. So I kept my conversation strictly on the new school and what I thought folks here, in this Southern "black belt" needed most to know. I was really surprised that he was interested in my ideas.

"What a uniquely refreshin' idea," he said about one of my suggestions.

"I would like to invite you for tea soon," he continued.

"I can tell you more about the plans for the Normal School and you can tell me more about Granville," he said, to my utter delight.

So, his first night in town was a big success. His first impression was good and he knew that if he was really gonna make an impression on this Southern town, then he was startin' out at the right place, the Judd Outlaw mansion.

Everybody knew the Outlaw family. We were known as far north as Delaware. A part of our family tree came from there. That was the part directly related to Mama Tutu, and although Judd Outlaw refused to accept it, it was so. Papa did not permit any conversation in his house about her Delaware and Virginia ancestors. For him, the Outlaw family only had one set of ancestors and they were his. Mama Tutu wasn't studin' Papa and she kept her family ties, tied tight. It was lucky for me that she did.

"I'm mighty obliged to you for your hospitality, Mr. Outlaw," Mr. Washington said, now addressin' Papa.

"You know, young man, my father, his father, his father's father, and his father's father's father were all farmers," Papa said. "A farmer has the job of growin' things and one generation teaches the next."

Papa had some point comin' up, I could tell, and Mr. Washington listened patiently with the utmost respect.

"Now you, you seem to think that farmin' is a science. You act like you can trick nature or somethin'," Papa continued.

"When I look over the fields you know what I see?"

"No, sir," Mr. Washington responded politely.

"I see sweat. I see bones breakin' in the sun. I see tears when rain breaks the drought and I can still see my Papa's hand steadyin' the hoe.

"Do you want to know the most important thin' I learned from my papa?" he asked.

"Yes, sir, I do," Mr. Washington then responded, leanin' in close.

"I learned that you reap what you sow. You know what I mean, son?" Papa said, leanin' closer to Mr. Washington.

"Why certainly, sir," he responded with an approvin' smile.

"We had to break our backs, but you, you betta' watch yours," Papa warned.

Then Papa took Mr. Washington under his wing. He draped his arm around his shoulders and quietly revealed some confidences that seemed to begin their close relationship. As the party continued at the Judd Outlaw estate, the two men talked for hours. Mama Tutu poked her head into the drawin' room and noticed that Papa was displayin' his rifle collection. She was so happy to see them gettin' along and she rushed off to the kitchen to fetch tea for them both.

"Can I get you gentlemen some biscuits?" she asked, sittin' the tea tray down on the walnut coffee table. I was perched on a footstool, behind the archway, within earshot of them.

"Stuffed," said Mr. Washington, puttin' his hand on his stomach.

Papa turned to her and said, "As soon as you finish in the kitchen, why don't you show Mr. Washington to his room. And please tell my wife to stop countin' the silver, for God's sake."

He knew that was what Mama did after havin' a house full of church folk for tea. Papa turned to Mr. Washington and whispered, "People who ain't never been poor don't know how to have things."

What he meant was that Mama's fortune had come easy. She was the only heir of an estate of her great-great-grandfather. Rumor had it that he was a white judge who had relations with a free woman of color before the Civil War. I recall hearin' the story about how his youngest brother inherited his likin' for what they used to jokingly call "brown sugar." The law kept him from marryin' any of them.

Josh's father was possibly one of those children, which would explain why Josh arrived with only his mother and two sisters and never a mention of his mother's husband.

Mama Tutu was the only family member that knew everythin' about the Virginia relatives, but talk of them was forbidden, and because she respected Papa's house, she never mentioned them around him. I was always askin' her questions and Mama Tutu took a likin' to tellin' me all the family secrets. My mama had a cousin who lived in France and was fathered by the younger brother of Mama's grandfather. Besides having the sugar cane plantation, much of the wealth that passed down the generations remained in the family and fell from that family tree.

Mama Tutu told me that before the Civil War it was safer to keep a family's wealth in the form of possessions rather than in currency. Property ownership and bank notes were not privy to colored people, so wealth was transferred through generations in the form of gold, silver, imported china, or other valuable objects, some of which adorned the guest room where Mr. Washington was stayin'. So Judd Outlaw's house was chock full of treasures, both in people and in things.

Mama Tutu took Mr. Washington through the house hissin' back and forth as they walked down the halls. Mama had originally planned to do the welcomin' but Mama Tutu insisted that she wanted to do the honors, so that gave me a chance to tag along. When she got to the guest room she put a key in the shinin' brass key plate and pushed the door open, leavin' the key inside.

"This is yours for as long as you wish," she said, smiling as she spoke.

He sighed deeply and looked into the bright clean room. The bed covers were almost luminous in the late afternoon sunlight. Brocade drapes arched the windows and hung down the frame to the floor. The white cotton spread which laid over the width and length of the huge oak bed had uniform cotton balls in lines across and down in rows which sunk into the wooden footboard. He looked to the left of the bed and a porcelain jug and basin sat upon the honey oak dressin' table. Both were lined with exquisite gold trimmin' and a colorful bouquet of flowers was painted inside a golden wreath on the face of the jug. In front of the wall to the right of the bed stood an oval mirror encased in a cherry wood frame, held in place by a stand made of the same strong wood and engraved with the pattern of a vine twistin' down the leg like a stem. The wide disc shaped base provided a deep contrast to the pinewood floors.

"What a lovely room," he said. "You may wish you hadn't said as long as I wished. I am not used to such splendor on the road. When I travel I am usually at the mercy of thieves."

"Well now you wit kin, and you can drop your guns," Mama Tutu said, with hearty laughter as she threw her arms around him once more. "You sho' is done to a turn!"

I could sense closeness between them. The rest of the week, whenever they were seen in the house together, they were whisperin' furiously. So whatever the connection, it was obvious that open discussion about it was not gonna happen in Judd's house. Once when I was carin' for the plants on the porch, I overheard one of their conversations through the drawin' room window. They were talkin' too low for me to hear the details of the conversation, but I was able to hear the name of Josh's mother mentioned.

I was not that interested in our family's roots. My only obsession was that I could have a chance to study at the Normal School and if there was a connection between my family and the Virginia families that left a remote possibility that I may be kin to the new schoolmaster. This would certainly guarantee me admission to the Normal School. I closed my eyes and prayed out loud, "Oh, God, please make it be so."

Chapter VII

The Dining Room

Even though it wasn't a cryin' time of day, I sat down at the dinin' room table and wept. So many conversations were held there. In my mind, I could see the smiles, feel the happiness, and taste the air full of the presence of my kinfolk. Sometimes hopeless faces hung low in despair around this table after repeated dark dry nights waitin' for rain. Then on mornin's when hope was nearly gone, we'd awaken to the sound of thunder and then rain beatin' on the rooftop. Once again, renewal was granted by an appeal to the ancestors I feel all round this table now. Is dey callin' me back? Is dey tryin' to give me a chance to straighten out some of the mess come in and out of this room? Now that I can see in the twenty-twenty vision of my remembrance, I can see exactly what needs changin'. The trouble is I really can't change it and I'm not really sure I would want to if I could.

Today the Outlaw life pulses through my heart with the hope of a new generation that vibrates with the rhythm of freedom and I'm all that's left to pass it on to them. I wanted the freedom to be somebody just like Luke wants it today. Bein' ordinary wasn't an option. Back then it was Mr. Washington who saw somethin' in me when nobody else could. If Luke could see what I see, he'd know the Alabama legislature is a piece of cake. Slowly, as I faded in and out of consciousness, I saw faint images appear, fluid and transparent, until I was suddenly transported backward in time.

"Aunt Pansy!" Luke yelled from the porch.

"She can't hear us knocking," said Luke, turning to his companion.

"Sometimes she drifts off completely, especially when she goes into the dining room. I think we better go around the back. Don't be alarmed though, she may be a little testy if we wake her up. Whenever she is fetched back from the past, she doesn't like it."

"Whoa! What past?"

"You know, back in time when she met Mr. Washington."

"So your Aunt Pansy gets taken back to the days of her youth?"

"That's right."

"And how is that?"

Luke looked strangely at his companion. "Have you ever heard of Vodoun?"

"Voo who?" Luke's companion asked with a snicker.

"Now it's called Voodoo, but back in the day it was a religion called Vodoun. Let's sit down out back and I'll explain," Luke said.

The two friends quietly walked around the side of the house to the back porch, a place Lil' Luke used to go often on his way around to the front porch to look out for his Aunt Pansy's friend, Huckabuck Marie. Huckabuck Marie, who was the child of a runaway slave, walked like she was still running. Lil' Luke knew her footsteps by heart and would bolt around to the front just to catch her takin' a short cut into town through our estate.

"Sit here," Luke pointed out one of the tall-back white wicker rocking chairs. "I'll go in and grab a couple of glasses of sherry to wet your whistle while I give you a lesson in the ancient spiritual practices of my ancestors," Luke taunted.

He turned and walked away then looked over his shoulder with a mysterious grin.

"Oh yeah, you mean something like libations," Luke's companion replied jokingly.

"Oh, so you do know something, huh?"

He returned with the drinks and sat in the other rocker.

"You see, my grandfather's father was a free black man and wealthy land owner on an Island in the Caribbean. When my grandfather was traveling abroad he met my grandmother in France. At the time that they met they had two things in common: money and their language. So naturally they fell in love. My granddaddy eloped with my grandmother and brought her to America. Both families were in shock. The way I heard it, my granddaddy's family was devastated because they had not consulted the ancestors, as was the custom of the Vodoun. They feared for the safety of the couple, so Mama Tutu was sent to protect them."

"Protect them from what?"

"Well, from any dangers that may befall them because they had not been under the covering of the ancestors. You see, Mama Tutu was a mambo, which is a name given to female specialists who possess spiritual powers. She would be a bridge to the ancestors, allowin' them to cover the couple and their descendants. This is how they continued their service to the family Iwa," Luke continued.

"Iwa?"

"Yes, certain species of large trees that are especially sacred because they are believed to be the homes of spirits and the conduits through which spirits enter the world of living humans," Luke explained. "That dining room table is made of Iwa wood."

"Okay, now I'm getting the creeps," complained Luke's friend.

"So this is how Aunt Pansy can experience the past as though she is in the present. "Understand?" Luke asked.

"Not really. Let's be real quiet," replied Luke's companion.

"You mean so we can eavesdrop?" Luke asked.

"Yeah. We might get some fresh new ideas about that Washington gent she's always boasting about."

"Absolutely. You'll be surprised what you can learn by not interrupting her flow. One of these days I'm going to plant myself under the table and write down every word she says. It gets pretty complicated when she speaks for every family member though. How she remembers what everyone said is a mystery that will go with her to her grave. This may be awhile since it looks as though she's determined this time to re-live her whole life over again.

"How does she remember all that?" Luke's companion asked.

"She sees the faces around that table. Faces of the people she had to fight for the right to be the person she became. She actually started a revolution in her time."

"I remember, as a young boy, the sight of her used to give me an erection," Luke said blushingly. "She was powerful and she could give scientific orations in her day, and now all she does is sit in the dining room and talk to ghosts."

"I bet we could listen a while if we hide in the closet under the stairs," said Luke's friend.

"We ain't gotta hide. She can't see anything when she starts to go back. We could stand on her stomach and she wouldn't notice."

"In that case, pour some more drinks. I think I'm going to sit back and enjoy the history lesson," Luke's friend responded.

"I'd not waste my time, if I were you. She doesn't really get the point. There is a war at stake, an election looming over us, and she's still livin' the high life of her youth."

"No matter, pass me the sherry; I've nothing to lose," said Luke's friend, going into the hallway and curling up in the closet like a field cat in a lingerie drawer.

"I'll be in the study composing my acceptance speech," Luke called out over his shoulder.

"You better write a concession speech too," replied his companion.

"Oh, thanks," said Luke. "Don't forget you said that when I'm making appointments!" The two men laughed out loud and Luke's Aunt Pansy started right in on a conversation.

"Hey, Luke, she's sitting at the table talking to the headmaster from that old Normal School. Is that the one where she used to teach?" Luke's companion asked.

"Oh you'll be there a while," replied Luke. "That's one of her favorite memories. She didn't just teach there. Hopefully she'll tell the whole story. Sometimes she can, sure 'nuff, see him in the flesh. It scares me when she starts talking to him though. I think I'll take myself a nap after I write the speech. Wake me up when you've had enough."

Chapter VIII

A Post Office Collision

Yes suh, that was the day we crashed like two meteors out of the sky. I knew them puffy, billowin' clouds blowin' by my window was warnin' somethin' a comin'. When Mama Tutu woke me up at the crack of dawn that mornin', it was to remind me to post the letter of my application to the Normal School. The clouds were breakin' up just after sunrise with the brightest mixture of orange and gold pushin' through spaces of shredded pink skies. That was a sure sign of a bright day ahead. Later that mornin' I was rushin' down Main Street tryin' to be the first one in line at the post office.

You were waltzin' your way down Main Street ahead of me as if you were movin' gracefully to the symphony of the mornin' colors. People seemed to part the way as you passed them with yo' steady gate and giant steps. The mornin' sun shone luminous orange rays on your brow. Your reddish colored hair flickered with gold highlights as the sun drenched you from the top of your head to the shine on your boots. People watched from their store fronts as each magnificent step you took seemed to lay claim to the turf you traversed.

Hats were tippin', young ladies proudly displayin' their most refined curt-seys—even dogs were chasin' at your heels. 'Cross the street folks were a whis-perin', "That's him, Mr. Washington, come down to build us a school." You were the talk of the town even though it had only been several weeks since your arrival. Nothin' distracted you from your destination though. I guess you was deep in thought about buildin' that schoolhouse. I figured you was ex-pectin' an urgent piece of correspondence 'cause you were dead set on gettin' there early too. After spendin' weeks speakin' to church, nightclub, and hos-pital audiences (not that there was more than one of each in Granville), many folks knew who you was by you workin' so hard to raise the funds necessary to build the first normal school in our quiet little agricultural town. When you finally looked up and noticed how the people were standin' back and makin' way for you, I declare, you even became a little embarrassed. You seemed like an ordinary man, with humble beginnin's, who bowed down to this kind of respect. This was the only kind of situation that made you feel awkward. Why, Mr. Washington, you ain't never liked to be set apart from others. Sure it was a little easier to accept this treatment when you were addressin' an audience, but by then you hadn't yet grown accustomed to all that kind of attention in your private life. Yeah, you had a hard time at first, but as your popularity grew, you got used to it and it became a part of your daily life. With all that big stuff goin' on 'bout you, honey chile, you still remained just another plate here at Judd Outlaw's dinner table.

"Hey, Luke, she thinks she's talking straight to him, like he's sitting with her at the table," Luke's companion yelled out from his hiding place in the closet.

"I told you, you don't even have to hide," Luke yelled back. "She's completely gone back. Enjoy! I hear her starting up again."

On that day though, I remember, you picked up yo' pace, avoidin' the curiosity of the crowd, so you could be the first to line up for the post office. Your childhood poverty musta made you shy, yet it propelled you far beyond the limitations of your class and color. With that brilliant mulatto skin and sparklin' red crown of hair, you stood out like a pumpkin in a tackle shop.

To keep up, I had to lift up my skirt with all its ruffles and undergarments. You weren't alone then, and I know I'm not alone now. I remember when you slowed down to have a look over your shoulder and I had a chance to catch my breath. I think you felt like you was bein' followed, so you began to take long fast strides. Sho' enough, I had to increase from a skip to a full-length canter. You hadn't been in town long enough to have creditors or love-torn misses, so you had no idea that I was the one followin' you. When we reached the post office doorway, I, in the grand style of a rapidly pursuin' admirer, intercepted your entrance to grab open the door for you. I didn't quite get my hand on the doorknob and my foot missed the first step. I musta been a site sprawled face down across the entire doorway. I still remember how embarrassed you were. I bet you can't remember how much you kept apologizin' and blamin' yo' self for bein' in such a rush. I can see it right now.

"Hey Luke, I think she's drifting way back," Luke's companion yelled.
"She's already there, if that loud yelling didn't wake her," Luke responded.
Pansy continued in her reverie.

"I'm terribly sorry, missus', I must mind my steps. It was inexcusably rude for me to block your entrance to the door. Will you please accept my humble apologies, my dearest missus?"

We were both stunned, I from the fall and you from the fear that you had caused me harm. I was still busy tryin' to regain the composure I had lost several blocks before when I started runnin' to keep up with you. Since you hit the ground runnin' in Granville, I hadn't had my chance to be with you. This was not the kind of first encounter I had hoped for, but at that point I decided to make the best of it. Yeah, we were meant to meet, you and me. I hear 'ya callin' me 'ole buddy. Let me just rest awhile.

"Hey, she's laying her head down on the table now. Is she all right?" Luke's friend again yelled up the stairs.

"Oh yeah, she's all right; she's just finding her way back. That's how she visits them. Haven't you noticed she becomes the voice of the persons in her past? She talks herself into a time travel and then slips into a deep sleep. If her head's down, she's gone now. You may as well come on up and help me with this speech."

"Good mornin' suh, uh, Mr. Washington, suh. I'm so sorry, suh. No need you apologizin' suh. Please forgive me," I begged.

"My gracious, missus, I'm terribly sorry," Mr. Washington replied.

"Oh no, no suh, it was my fault entirely, uh...uh, it was me... I...I...I shouldn't 'a, well, I..., I was gonna', I mean you were here befo'...well, I guess we both..., I mean....," I was standin' there stammerin'.

"Never mind," Mr. Washington responded very gently, caressin' my tremblin' hand.

"Now you just make sure you're all right, that's all that matters now, missy," he smiled.

That's when we both leaned over to pick up the envelope that I had dropped durin' the fall. Mr. Washington reached out and grabbed my chin to avoid a head-to-head collision.

"Now you just settle down, missus, I'll get that." Again he smiled, but this time our eyes met and I blushed with embarrassment. I was feelin' completely humiliated and belittled and all at the same time feelin' as if I had received an injection of some high potency elixir. A current of magnetic energy passed from his eyes into my soul. I stood up dumbfounded and elated.

"Oh thank you, suh, thank you very kindly," I said as I curtsied.

"Now careful, missus, are you steady there?" he asked.

"Oh yes, suh, Mr. Washington," I said, slightly intoxicated by his presence. He handed me the envelope and walked into the post office.

"Excuse me, suh, may I impose on you just a moment more?"

"As you wish, missus, but just a moment, I have important business to attend to this mornin'," he replied.

"I know, suh, you see I am the grand-niece, once removed, of the right reverend whose letter you are here to fetch."

A sudden look of surprise crossed his face.

"Oh, please, excuse me, suh, I didn't mean to pry, or should I say, I wasn't snoopin' around. I just happened to hear Mama Tutu sayin' that she know for sure that huh sista's husband, the right reverend, was preparin' his response to your request and that it would be in the post by Wednesday mornin' straight from Virginia, where he went to make sure the property deed is all legal. And this is Wednesday mornin', ain't it, Mr. Washington?" I asked.

But before Mr. Washington could answer, I continued.

"Yes, suh, and since it is Wednesday mornin' I just reckon that you'd be out to fetch the mail bright and early, right, suh?"

"Well…"

But before he could say anythin', I kept on talkin'.

"And since you was spectin' the most important letter for you, I decided to mail the most important letter for me, on the same day," I babbled on. "At the same time I was tryin' hard to get a chance to make my acquaintance with my future headmaster, suh."

My voice had practically reached a harsh penetratin' shrill by then. I was pantin' for my breath and I was still goin' on. "That's of course, suh, if my application is accepted by the Mr. Colonel, suh. up there in the North Country, suh, where you come from, suh, right, suh?"

"It's General, missus, General."

"Yes, suh, I mean the one done send you down here suh to open up the Normal School, suh. That's of course, suh, if the right reverend, my uncle suh, once removed that is, will give the okay for the church congregation to agree, suh. I just know he gonna' give his support to the capital fund raisin' campaign, suh. It's fo' sho, you know, suh, 'cause when I was listenin' to Mama Tutu tellin' my mama she had the sound of confidence in her voice. This here letter, suh, that I'm sendin' out here today…" I stood there jumpin' up and down and wavin' the letter in Mr. Washington's face, "I'm sendin' out on account of the sound of certainty that I heard in Mama Tutu's voice."

"Now hold on to your bonnet and just you wait a minute, little missus," he said authoritatively. "You be better off not sticking your nose into old folks business. But since you done it already this time, I sure hope what you heard is the truth before God," he added.

Mr. Washington had turned toward the post office, when I called out to him. "You can bet more on Mama Tutu than you can on God," I said with a big confident smile.

Mr. Washington whirled around and I was hoisted up the two steps with his strong hands clasped around my waist. "If you believe in Mama Tutu, I will too!"

Just then I started to feel the loneliness creepin' over me like a spider's web. At least the memories linger, better to be able to remember. Wait, what's that?

"I hears footsteps. Must be Luke comin' back from his meetin'."

"I hears four feet. Shhhh. Quiet down, memories, somebody's comin.'"

"Aunt Pansy, you still awake?"

Luke's companion was checking to see if she was aware of the conversations she was keeping. He tiptoed past the dining room to go upstairs and see what Luke had to say about it. Luke didn't seem at all concerned.

"Come on, I'll show you. She won't even respond once she drifts off. Can't convince her she's not building that schoolhouse all over again."

"Let's go out the back or we'll wake her," offered Luke's friend.

"Oh she's not asleep. She's just in a trance. You heard it for yourself. Not a soul in there. But to hear her, you'd think the whole family walked right out of their graves and filled this house again. When she sits at the dining table she sees everybody then. Some days she carries on for hours in there. Go on back to your hideout in the closet. The best is yet to come.

"Must not've been Luke after all," I'm thinkin' as I drifted back to that day.

"Like I was sayin', suh, you didn't have a resident address yet in Granville, and so you had to use a post office box."

When we arrived at the post office it was just openin' for the day. It was eight o'clock sharp.

"Good mornin' sir." said the man behind the counter who poked out his chest to make sure that you saw the badge settin' high on the breast pocket of his shirt.

"Good mornin', Sheriff," replied Mr. Washington.

"Oh, I'm not the sheriff; I'm just the deputy," he replied.

Cotton was plentiful in Alabama, but not buildin's, so the post office and the sheriff's office were one in the same.

"Thirty-three Granville Place, please," said Mr. Washington.

He didn't really need to say the address because you could see the mansion from the center of town, poised at the top of Main Street, and everyone knew he was stayin' there.

The deputy turned to me, "Why, good mornin' to you, too, Miss Pansy."

I tipped my head without sayin' anythin'. The deputy called out behind the huge walnut counter to the postmaster's assistant.

"Jake, you got a customer. Come on out here, boy."

Jake came right out and put a stack of mail on the counter in front of Mr. Washington.

"Mornin', sir, I was just sortin' the drop from Virginia; it arrived a little late this mornin'," he said. "I can't see anythin' for you in this here mornin' batch so far, I'm afraid. Maybe when I finish sortin' through the late stack that came, I'll find what you lookin' fo'," he continued.

Mr. Washington was a little disappointed I could tell, but then he turned to me and I was still just as confident as ever.

"Well, here, Mr. Jake," I said, handin' him my envelope. "You make sure this letter gets on that pony today, Jake. You hear? When you find Mr. Washington's letter in your stack, put your flag out and I'll come back and fetch it for him."

I looked at Mr. Washington and gave him a big, confident, sweet Southern smile, and he smiled back, tippin' his hat to me. I dashed for the door, in a hurry to double check with Mama Tutu about the latest word from Virginia. In Granville, good 'ole church gossip traveled ten times faster than the Pony Express.

"Watch your step, young lady," I heard a voice call after me.

"Yes, suh!" I responded like I was followin' military orders.

I was so glad the sheriff wasn't the one to give Mr. Washington temporary accommodations. He had offered to share his room above the post office with him. It was very difficult for an educator like Mr. Washington to find comfort in the home of a former Confederate soldier. At the first dinner we had at our house, Papa made Mr. Washington sit at the other head of the table. That's when Papa said he'd be better off sleepin' in his grave than stayin' with a man done killed to keep him a slave. Mr. Washington is the only man to this day big enough to sit facin' opposite Judd Outlaw at the head of his table and not be intimidated.

The correspondence that did arrive later that day was from 'da General to 'da sheriff. It was the announcement, already old news to Mr. Washington, that one of the church families had offered him hospitality while he was in Granville. Another example of how gossip travels faster than the pony. The letter from General Armstrong also gave full endorsement of the proposal to build the Normal School by the Colored Methodist Church and Reverend Daniel L. Pickett. Reverend Pickett further stated that he, through the power and choice of his congregation, is lendin' his full support to the capital fund raisin' campaign. He also guaranteed the cooperation of other faith communities, which had already began to spread the news of this noble endeavor in their congregations. So on the evenin' of the near catastrophic encounter with me, Mr. Washington found himself bein' introduced by my uncle (once removed), the honorable right reverend Daniel L. Pickett, by letter, to Mama Tutu as his hostess durin' the time of his stay at the Outlaw estate. He didn't know that he was already well into his second week with us thanks to Mama Tutu.

The followin' day I was sweepin' the porch early so I could finish my chores and have more time to read. Mama Tutu kept a close watch on my duties around the mansion. I also wanted to write up the changes I observed in several of the plants I had perched on the railin' facin' the risin' sun. Just as I was mixin' in the soil, I spotted Huckabuck Marie, comin' toward the porch.

"Good mornin', Miss Pansy. Word has already gotten around," she said as she briskly walked toward me.

"Word of what?"

"Word...you know what I mean. I've already heard that the gentleman, Mr. Washington from Virginia, is stayin' here with you. Is that true, dear?"

I didn't bother to look up from my little pot of dirt and Huckabuck Marie continued talkin'.

"Well, you know, I happen to know some mighty important information about General Armstrong. You know, the person who done sent him down here." She continued, "Yes'm, I reckon he be very happy to hear what I know. I just know he's waitin' furious for a letter from him. So why don't you be a perfect darlin' and arrange a meetin' between me and him and I'll make sure he stays one up on the whole town, and I got it straight from the horse's mouth. I 'spect you got about as close a contact with him as anybody in this house. I mean, you bein' so interested in them plants and things."

I stopped and looked up from my work on the porch.

"Don't think I can't see some things when I'm walkin' by here to my job and back past here every day. I do notice things, you know," she said.

"That's mighty nice of you to notice, mame."

"Don't call me mame, chile, I ain't but nine years your senior and that don't make me no mame to you."

"I'm sorry, mmm..." I caught myself before I finished the word and we both laughed. "Well, what should I call you?"

"I don't much care what you call me. Just don't call me late for dinner!" We both laughed again. "Why don't you call me Huck," she said. "Most everybody else does, 'cept they don't mean nothin' good when they do. Don't think I don't knows how they be talkin' bout me, and it don't bother me none. I know who I am and what I'm doin'. Ain't got no need to please eva'body. Yeah, that'll be fine, you jus' call me Huck, Miss Pansy. That'll suit me."

"How do you know my name?"

"Eva'body knows who you are. You and your whole family," she responded.

"Well, I like your uniform, Huck. It's quite becomin'," I remarked.

"Yeah, I like it my se'f, but I won't be wearin' it for long," she said.

"Already got your notice?" I asked.

"No, I ain't gettin' notice this time. This time it's me givin' notice. In my twenty-three years of life I ain't never seen a bunch of men any rougher than those stagecoach men. They ain't got no respect for a lady like me, and before I knock one of them out, I beta' be leavin'. That's the other reason why I want to meet Mr. Washington. 'Cause when I heard about the school comin' to Granville, I know they gonna need somebody to take care of the office and maybe if I'm the first to ask him, he'll give me the job. There's got to be somethin' for eva'body once that school is up, so don't you forget about that meetin', okay, Ms. Pansy? I gotta' rush on to work now but I'll stop by on my way home for the answer. Remember to tell him it's about the General!"

When Huckabuck Marie came back pass the house I was out tendin' my plants on the porch again. I ran down to the street to meet her and slipped her a note. The note which was addressed to "Miss Huckabuck" explained the day and time that was suitable for her and Mr. Washington to meet. She took the note in stride like an Olympic runner receivin' a baton, without lookin' to the left or the right.

Later that night she opened and read it. It said, "I will be delighted to share in your company one week from today at 6 P.M. at the location of your choice."

Huckabuck Marie couldn't believe she got her one chance to meet with Mr. Washington. I was happy for her too, and I said a little prayer knowin' her reputation.

"Please, God, don't let her blow it."

The next week was the week before the Independence Day celebration in Granville. Huck knew that if she played her cards right that she would get her ticket to ride right off that stagecoach line. That afternoon, I had a feelin' that somehow by his hand our lives would be forever linked. Huckabuck Marie returned a note to him by me explainin' where they should meet. She knew not to try to meet Mr. Washington at the Outlaw house. What was familiar to her was rather common in comparison. She worried it may not be appropriate for a gentleman such as him, yet the saloon was the best place for her. She told him, in the note, that no reply from him would mean that it was okay.

When that day came she was so excited that she arrived a half-hour early for the appointment and was sittin' in the corner booth facin' the door. She watched the strands of smoke floatin' through the sunbeams and kept her eyes peeled to the door. Although there was no music at the time, she nervously patted out a ragtime melody with her foot. It was much later that I learned that was her way of managin' fear. No other outward sign of fear was noticeable. Doc Holiday, the bar keeper, recognized her nervous habit. He had seen it many times before and had suggested some gin and tonic to calm her down.

By 6:00 P.M. sharp, she had swallowed enough tar water to be feelin' no fear when Mr. Washington walked through the saloon doors. Everybody's eyes turned his way. The doors kept a background rhythm, swingin' on the hinges behind him with a hummin' sound rumblin's through the air. Little by little, as folks noticed him, one table after another hushed and became still.

His eyes searched the room for her. He stood tall and hard like a California redwood. Then he saw her across the room leanin' forward on her elbow, flutterin' her fingers to motion him forward. When it captured his attention, their eyes met, he touched the brim of his Stetson lightly and bowed his head. He started walkin' toward the table where she sat. When he reached it he removed his hat completely from his head and with his famous wide sweepin' gesture and an even deeper bow, he greeted her.

"Howdy do, mame. I expect you must be Miss Huckabuck?"

"Yes, suh, that's me," slowly and deliberately she replied.

"Well, it's mighty nice to make your acquaintance, madame."

Huck didn't like any formalities, but the sound of madame from his cultured lips sent goosebumps down her spine.

"Well I'm not much for words, Mr. Washington," she said, "and I suppose you must be in a big hurry to hear the news I have about the General."

He pointed down to the seat at the booth where she was sittin'.

"Do you mind?" he asked.

"Oh, by all means, please have a seat, Mr. Washington. I didn't mean to forget my manners."

Now I know enough about Huckabuck Marie to know that manners definitely played second fiddle to her theme. Whenever she remembered them it was usually after the fact. Yet her beauty and charm made up for the absence of etiquette in most instances. The way I got the story, straight from the horse's mouth, she launched right into the matter at hand.

"There are two things I want to talk with you about. One is the news, what Pansy Outlaw gave you the note fo'. The other thing is a question, a kinda' favor. As I said I'm not too good with words, but sometimes, yeah, sometimes I can get a feelin' about somethin' and sure enough it happens."

"Is the news about General Armstrong one of those feelings?" he asked.

"Oh no, suh, that ain't no feelin', that's fact. You see, I work down at the stagecoach junction. Some days they have me collectin' boardin' passes and other days they have me sendin' them. When they's real important, they sends them by Pony Express. So last week they had me send a stagecoach pass by Pony Express to General Armstrong and I heard them talkin' somethin' about a ground breakin'. Now I don't know what a ground breakin' is, but I do know it's gonna happen right here in Granville.

"Are you sure?" asked Mr. Washington with grave interest.

"Like I said, I'm not sure what a ground breakin' is, but I know for sure I sent him two passes, one for him and one for his missus. They's comin' to Granville one month from today."

"Well, sir—err, I mean, madame. This is good news." Mr. Washington then reached into his pocket.

"Let me give you something for your time, madame."

"No, suh, that won't be necessary," Huck quickly responded.

She took another big gulp of the tonic and slowly lowered the glass to the table. She wasn't much of a drinker, so that gulp went straight to her head. She lowered the glass and tried to focus her eyes on Mr. Washington's face 'til the two faces she was seein' finally returned to one. She began to speak.

"What I was really hopin', suh, is that I could ask you one favor."

"Of course. Just name it, madame, and the good Lawd and I will find a way somehow. After all, already in the short time I've known you, you have given me the hope I needed to carry on."

"Well suh, if the good Lawd see fit for you to build the school you come down here to build, then I reckon' you gonna' need somebody for the office work. Since I been workin' at the stagecoach junction I got pretty good at schedulin' things. I do a real good job keepin' records of when a coach is comin' in and when one is goin' out. I'm the one who made up the chart where they post all the trips for da whole month. That's another reason I knows when the general is comin'. So what I'm sayin', suh..."

"It's fine, Miss Hu... Huu... Huckabuck, it's fine," he stuttered.

"It's Huckabuck Marie, suh. I know it's a funny name, but it's my mamma's name. See she used to like to dance a lot and do the Huckabuck, so round here, once you get a nickname, it stays with you forever. So when I was born, my mamma named me Marie and my daddy called me Huckabuck Marie after my mamma. So that name done stayed with me. If it's too much trouble for you, suh, you can jus' drop the Huckabuck.'

"No, no, madame, not at all, Huckabuck Marie is what it is and Huckabuck Marie is what it'll be."

He put out his hand, smiled, and said, "When the school office opens, I'll expect you to be there."

"Oh yes, suh, thank you, suh. Thank you, thank you, thank you, suh. I didn't know what I was gonna' do, if I had to work the rest of my life at the stagecoach junction."

They both stood up and with the handshake the contract was signed. Huckabuck Marie was beamin' from the great news and her hope of a new beginnin'. Mr. Washington was also happy, because if General Armstrong was comin' to Granville for a ground breakin', then that was definitely a sign of his commitment to and support for the project.

The next day I was waitin' on the porch for Huckabuck Marie to come by. After I snipped leaves and untangled branches, I added a little of my home-made soil mixture to each pot and patted it into the moist soil. I had done all this to the plants the day before but I had to do somethin' rather than just stand idle on the porch. Mama Tutu would not allow any of her girls to hang outdoors, lessen' they was doin' a chore. She always said that that was a totally low life thing to do and that any lady of her house would not be caught dead standin' outside. I always wondered when she said that how anyone could be dead and still standin'. It always got a howlin' laughter out of little Luke any time he heard her say that. Mama Tutu filled this world richly with posthumous comments. Her words would last long after she was gone.

Finally, a few days later, I saw Huckabuck Marie comin' down the road. She had a walk that could not be mistaken. I waived my handkerchief in the air to beckon her. I couldn't call out to her for fear Mama Tutu would notice. Huckabuck Marie was on Mama Tutu's condemned list.

"What happened, what'd he say?" I asked with a loud whisper as she came closer.

"Why didn't you tell me he was so handsome?" answered Huckabuck Marie.

"I almost lost my nerve; had to have Doc Holiday mix me a tonic. Do you know, he called me madame and I almost fainted? The sound of his voice is like potion on an open wound—you know it's healin' you, but it stings like thunder. I didn't dare tell him I weren't no madame!"

Huckabuck Marie just stood there starin' off into the clouds.

"Yeah, yeah.. and what did he say?" I blurted out impatiently.

"He said yes."

"He said yes what?"

"He said, 'When the school office opens, I'll expect you to be there,'" responded Huckabuck Marie in a semi-daze.

That conversation got on my nerves so bad I wanted to spit. It took all my self-control to not grab her by the shoulders and shake her silly. She had an awful glazed look in her eyes and I began to think she had been by to see Doc Holiday on the way over.

"Will you please snap out of it and talk in English!" I screamed.

Huckabuck Marie seemed to be intoxicated or somethin'. I wanted details and she knew quite well there was no school and certainly there was no office.

"I'm hired to work in the office," she said in a sing-song tone.

"Office, what office are you talkin' about?"

"The Normal School office," she said, still talkin' like she was halfcocked.

"What are you talkin' about, there is no school yet!" I screamed.

I startled Huckabuck Marie right out of her dream, and she quickly looked down at her gold timepiece.

"Oh Lawd, I'm gonna to be late if I don't get."

Huckabuck just waved her hand at me and said, "I'll see you on the way back maybe, and thank you. Thank you so much." She took off like a scalded cat.

That evenin', the followin' evenin', and again the next after that I fiddled around outside with my plants. I never did see Huckabuck Marie passin' by. This angered me so. Why didn't she keep her promise and come? I plum ran out of excuses to be standin' out on the porch. I knew there had to be more to the story and I deserved to know. After all, I set up the meetin' and all. What if she knew somethin' about my chances of gettin' into the school? Wouldn't she tell me? Or didn't she care about anybody but herself? I needed answers and I needed them right away. I couldn't wait any longer and it was no tellin' when I would catch Huckabuck Marie passin' by again. So I made a plan.

Chapter IX

Meeting of the Minds

The followin' evenin' I wanted to go look for Huckabuck Marie, but I couldn't tell Mama Tutu that I had to care for the plants again. Mama Tutu knew enough about my project to know that once I've pruned them, packed the soil and watered them, there was no more to be done to them for a couple of weeks.

"You s'posed to let nature take its course," she said any time she saw me fussin' with them too much. So I decided that maybe if I invited Mr. Washington outside to show him my experiments I would have a chance to catch Huckabuck Marie as she was passin' by on her way home. I'd be feedin' two birds with one crumb. I could find out what the story was about the school and Huckabuck Marie would see what a special relationship I already had developed with Mr. Washington. So at dinner I rushed to sit near him at the table. He sat at the head and papa at the other head. I grabbed the corner seat next to him. Mama Tutu served a luscious dinner that night with two meats and many vegetable dishes gracin' the table. Right after the prayer, I leaned over the bowl of string beans to ask Mr. Washington, secretly, if he would like to see my scientific experiment with plants.

"I most certainly would, Miss Pansy," was his response.

That night for dessert Mama served one of my practice homemade pies. Unfortunately the pie didn't hold together from the pie pan to the plate. Mr. Washington mentioned how perfectly tart the blueberries were and how ever since he was a little kid he always enjoyed eatin' his pie with a spoon. I couldn't figure out whether he was just bein' kind or whether he was tellin' the truth. Perfectly tart, hmmm... I could never decide if that was good or bad either. At least tonight after dinner I would have a chance to share my true genius with him.

"I have twelve saplin's," I boasted, "all from seed and all treated with my special blend of soils."

"Your soils?" he inquired.

"Yes, suh, I'm still in the experimental stages."

"Oh really," he replied. "I am quite looking forward to seeing your work."

My work, he said—my work. Somethin' about that stuck with me. He and I withdrew from the table immediately after dinner. He showed so much excitement about seein' the results of my experiments that I thought he was pretendin'. Then he told me that he had done a similar experiment and had come up with a way of enrichin' soil by addin' other minerals. He said that he had not yet had a chance to test it on the kind of seed I had used for my experiments. He asked a ton of questions, and before we knew it, it was midnight.

Mr. Washington took out his tobacco and was packin' it in his corn pipe and I was curled up at his feet. I used an old rag rug that used to sit in front of the 'ole rocker, as a foot warmer, to sit upon. It didn't do much good keepin' the hard wood floor from pressin' against my hipbone. I described every test I had done with the plants. Mr. Washington listened vigorously while he jus' kep' on rockin' and puffin'. I told him of some of the things I was able to do to treat the sick animals. He wanted to know more and more.

I told him about the time when Papa Judd's mare gave birth to her first colt and how I'd slept in the barn all night that night, watchin' and waitin' as the night passed before my eyes, and how I could hear the dew hittin' the ground it was so quiet. Right before sunrise the mare started circlin' the stall. There wasn't anyone else awake and hardly a soul stirrin' for miles around. When I got up close she was kickin' the sideboards so hard it rattled the whole barn. I thought a hornet or somethin' stung her. I had just dozed off for a minute and I didn't know what had hit her. I was ready to take a little nap and her kickin' woke me up. She banged into the gate with both hoofs and one foot got caught. She fell over and couldn't move. I think maybe she twisted her leg when she fell. It was very hard to free her foot from the gate, but once I did, I saw the new colt comin' out from behind. I wanted to run into the house to get Papa, but the mare was on her side and it was hard for the colt to drop since the mare couldn't stand on the sore rear ankle, especially with the weight of the kid.

"Why didn't you yell for help?" he asked.

"I couldn't. I think I was in shock," I said.

"So what did you do next?" he probed.

"Well I grabbed the leg that was in the way of the colt's head and lifted it over my shoulder to hold it up so the colt could slip out," I said.

"Well, did it?" he asked.

"Oh yes, suh, she slipped out all right, but she didn't move and it looked like she wasn't breathin'."

"Yeah?" asked Mr. Washington, who was now sittin' at the edge of the rockin' chair and waitin' for my next words.

"Well, I looked around for somethin' to use, anythin'. I wanted to poor water or somethin' on her to wake her up, but when I looked around the barn all I saw was the fire starter over in the corner with some of Papa's tools. I rush over, picked it up, dipped it in the horse's trowel to shake the dust from the end of it and stuck it in the colt's mouth."

At this point I could see Mr. Washington had almost stopped breathin'.

"And what happened, Pansy?" he asked with such excited interest I almost couldn't continue. "Go on," he said.

"Well, suh, I began pumpin' air down her throat until I heard the screechin' noise of her squealin' voice fill the barn house. A few minutes later, it was amazin' watchin' her puny little legs struggle for a way to support her body and then the mare strugglin' along with her until they both stood up. The mare licked her new foal clean. I dropped to my knees completely exhilarated. The mare limped over to me. I was cryin' so hard I thought she was comin' over to lick me dry too, but instead she just gently nudged me with her head. I guess it was her way of sayin' thanks. Next I heard footsteps. When I stood up and looked, everybody was runnin' from the house toward the barn to find out why the mare was yelpin'. Papa, Mama, Mama Tutu, and Josh, all came runnin'. Lil' Luke wasn't born yet, but he can tell you the story like he was standin' right there since he heard it so many times."

"I guess he's lived it through you enough times now to have been there," said Mr. Washington lovingly.

"Actually, Josh used to always brag about me to him. I think he the one told him the story so many times. 'Make sure you listen to your big sister Pansy,' he would say. 'She knows a lot about a lot of things.'

"I can't believe Papa let them churchwomen take Josh away. He was a good boy. He ain't do nothin' but mind his manners and do his chores. But that's a whole notha story and my bum is hurtin' bad on this hard porch floor," I confessed.

"Sometimes grown-ups make decisions between themselves that intend to help," Mr. Washington said.

"But he ain't do nothin' wrong," I said.

"I didn't say he did," he replied.

"Then he shouldn't have had to leave. Papa was pleasin' them churchwomen that's all and that wasn't fair. That's not all either, after eighth grade Josh had to go work in the field. Now I hardly ever see him. It ain't right. He's livin' with some church folk that don't know nothin' about him. They ain't no kin. Nothin'. One day I'll show 'em. I got a mind to hitch up the 'ole mare and tare through there in the night to save him from that hellhole. I knows they's probably treatin' him like he a slave."

"Well, Miss Pansy I can see that you miss him," he said.

"I more than miss him, Mr. Washington. I owe him. And I'm gettin' him back. You mark my word. As I stand before God, under the heavenly stars, Josh can rest assured I won't let him down. Like I said, even if I have to fetch him myself."

Mr. Washington looked at me and smiled. It was a very kind smile. Not like he was seein' anythin' funny but more like he was agreein' with me. It was like he understood. It made me feel sure about somethin'. I was sure I had a true friend.

Huckabuck Marie never even passed by that night either. It was not that important anymore for me to know what she and Mr. Washington had discussed. What was important to me then was my relationship to him. It had begun on a good note and although he had made no promises to me regardin' the school, my devotion to him had already taken root. My behind on the other hand had stiffened like rock.

In the weeks ahead we established new tests for the soil. He showed me many ways to mix it. He also taught me more about animal husbandry. I developed an even stronger desire to become his student at the normal school. Teachin' me, he said, convinced him of his ability to teach. I was a good sample. If he could teach a student who had no basis on which to build the advance scientific concepts, then others were capable of learnin' them too. What he said I had was an indelible spirit and a thirst for knowledge. He told me if the other new students had just this quality alone, he would have no doubts about facin' the challenge ahead of him. He saw the success of the school's future. He saw my own personal success. He saw the success of his mission and the completion of his childhood dream. He saw all this and more, lookin' into my hungry eyes. It took me a long time before I could begin to see what he saw that day.

Chapter X

540 Acres of Land

By 1888 the school had not only been built but was spread out over 540 acres of land. It was fully enrolled with both men and women students. The sale of bricks raised some of the money for new buildin's. The bricks had been fired in the kiln by one of the first freshmen classes. It was a full-fledged trainin' academy.

Enthusiasm continued to rise among the town's people for such skilled trades as carpentry, cabinetmakin', printin', shoemakin', and tin smithin'. Boys studied farmin' and dairyin' while girls learned all these plus cookin' and sewin'. Student labor supplied a large part of the resources for the school. Mr. Washington had married his third wife by then and she was in charge of admissions. She was an excellent business partner, completely confident in her abilities and unshaken in her devotion to her husband. I never understood how she never felt threatened by the women who flanked him wherever he went. I think she knew that her survival with him depended on the freedom he felt. She granted him that freedom willingly. It seemed harder for us to leave him be than it did for her. We wanted to protect him and possess him from all the others. He was a magnet for men, women, and children. She simply went about her business assiduously, as if her love bubble would never burst. She adored him and she also loved farmin', and that made her feel right at home in Granville.

Granville was a farmin' town and there had been a rather long dry season that year. Mr. Washington had started showin' some of the younger boys, who thought they was too good for farmin', how to make what he called "the strongest brick in the South." He put the other older boys to work fertilizin' the soil. He gave them long skinny glass bottles and made them collect small bits of the soil in them, mix it with some water, and cook it over a fire. We all thought he was makin' some kind of medicine. He kept records of everythin' he did. I saw him writin' down letters and numbers before pourin' the mixtures back into each of the four squares of dirt he had placed in a box on the side of the porch directly under the late afternoon sun. He was always tryin' to figure somethin' out, but when that ole Huckabuck Marie came swingin' her hips down the street, that man would stop whatever he was doin'.

Most of the time, he would tip his big brown wide brimmed hat and simply say "Howdy do, madame." Eva 'body know'd she wasn't no madame. One thing Granville folk was sure about, even if they had to die tryin', was to keep dey's socializin' as far from anywhere 'ole Huckabuck Marie ever was or had ever been.

Her daily walk down Main Street was one of the main events of the day. The town women were as green as collards with the envy they had toward her and none of them knew exactly why they hated her so. Mr. Washington ignored all the warnin' he got.

One day when Mama Tutu and Mr. Washington was sittin' on the porch drinkin' some of Mama Tutu's famous lemonade, she come struttin' by.

"She's either lookin' for a job or goin' to work," laughed Mama Tutu, "and whichever it is the next time you see her, she'll be doin' the opposite. That child tries to work an honest job, but every job she gets she can't keep. She don't last a minute soon as the boss's wife gets a look at huh, the next day she be gettin' her walkin' papers. She don't have a clue and most times it ain't nothin' wrong with how she does the job. Her problem comes from dat walk and those feed bags she's carryin' in front of her."

Mr. Washington just scratched the top of his head and then placed his hat back on it. He gave Mama Tutu a curious smile and I noticed a kind of sparkle in his eyes.

"I sho' hope you got enough sense to know trouble when you sees it," Mama Tutu said to him.

"What exactly is this madame's crime," he asked?

"She don't have to commit no crime; it's a sin just lookin' at her."

"Oh, I see. she hasn't been involved in any trouble in town. She just looks like trouble. Is that it?" Mr. Washington asked.

"Call it whatever you want, Mr. Washington, but when she ain't walkin' down the street struttin' her stuff, she is spendin' time at the Doc Holiday saloon in town. Now I don't know what you call it, but in my day, weez called them 'ladies of the night' and that ain't never been no compliment," Mama Tutu scoffed.

Mr. Washington went back to writin' notes on his note pad. He quickly decided that Mama Tutu wasn't ready to know that Huckabuck Marie was employed at the normal school and that her manner and her looks had both been inspirational and refreshin' to him, which provided a significant contrast to the strict and pedantic environment of academia.

I had come to know her in a good light also. She was always encouragin' me about my studies. She often offered to help me study and, in return, I would invite her for supper. Mama Tutu was never pleased on those occasions and had no problem expressin' her displeasure.

It was on one of those occasions that I really felt bad for her.

"Some folks affect a soul like a hurricane does the countryside, wipes out everythin' along its path," Mama Tutu said.

She looked straight across the table at Huckabuck Marie when she said it. I was so busy clearin' the table, I didn't notice if she responded or not. Knowin' her, she was so used to comments like that directed toward her from Mama Tutu she didn't even bat an eye. I'm the one who winced and caught the attention of Mr. Washington, who was leanin' back so as to loosen the buckle on his trousers without too much notice. Papa was the one who came to her defense in such a way that Mama wouldn't feel jealous and Mama Tutu would stop the attack.

"Hurricanes are the sort of thing the land needs once in a while. Without which, Mama Tutu, we'd all be dyin' from malaria or some other dreadful parasite nestin' in the swamps all summer," he said.

"I hope after this long, hot, dry summer you ain't loss your enthusiasm, Mr. Washington?" Papa asked. I want you to know, this daughter of mine," Papa pointed to me, "don't much like kitchen work. She's fittin' to finish her scientific education at the new school. I bet b'fo you know, she'll be curin' diseases that we ain't never even heard of yet," he said with a thunderous laugh.

Papa's confident laughter immediately removed the tension in the air.

"But before you get too big for your britches, do you think you can get your papa a cup of coffee to help digest this fine meal?" he asked.

"Yes, suh," I said, and eyed Huckabuck Marie, motionin' with my head for her to come and help me in the kitchen.

The table talk was as fertile as compost that night. I knew it would be easier to listen to it from the other room. Sure as summer follow spring, if you leave the grown-ups at the dinner table, at the Outlaw mansion, the conversation will get spicy. While the coffee was perkin' we'd be perched on the kitchen counter with our glasses pressed against the wall for earphones.

"I don't know why you so hard on that gal, Mama Tutu," Papa said.

"Look, I don't mind us reachin' out to the sinners in our community, but do we have to have them at dinner?" she protested.

"Hold on now," said Papa. "Aren't we taught that he who is without sin should cast the first stone?"

Then my Mama chimed in. She had more to say about Huckabuck Marie than she had to say the whole night about anythin'—startin' from the damagin' influence she believed she to have on me to stories she heard from the deaconess board.

"She's a woman can't be trusted in the privacy of our home. I mean, I never."

Mama became very upset. Eva'body was talkin' at once so it was difficult to hear over the noise. Mama Tutu spoke to Mr. Washington who had been carefully avoidin' the whole conversation and was simply collectin' all the dinner plates in one stack makin' a clangin' sound.

"What would you do with a cheap whore like her who thinks she is one of us?" asked Mama Tutu.

"I beg your pardon, ma'am?" he replied.

"You heard me right, and I'm bein' as nice as I can 'cause we got company."

"Well, I don't really know that I would go so far as to say anythin' derogatory about Ms. Huckabuck Marie since nothin' of my acquaintance with her has given me that kind of impression," remarked Mr. Washington.

By then, while the adults were in heated discussion, the two younger children had surely slipped out of their seats and were playin' hide and seek under the table. I was bustin' with embarrassment and accidently knocked over a glass that crashed to the floor. Papa started hollerin' at Lil' Luke and Josh thinkin' they had caused somethin' to fall from the other end of the table. Then he ordered Lil' Luke to go and see what was takin' the coffee so long. Then I didn't hear Mama anymore because she returned to her indigo silence. I wish I could have seen her face. Huckabuck Marie and I started clamorin' around with the cups and saucers to act like we were busy gettin' coffee. But I knew she was hurt. She was hurt bad, I could tell. She tried to pick up the glass and her hand got a little cut. She brushed it off against her red plaid dress. I waved my hand toward the coffee to hurry her along and take her mind off the insults.

"Hey Luke!" cried out Luke's companion.

"Yeah," Luke replied.

"The old lady's gone off to sleep."

"She's not asleep," Luke said.

"Quiet down," Luke warned, "you're gonna break the spell. She'll be like that for hours. Don't try to talk to her though. She got plenty company now. You might as well take up a regular chair at the table with her. Shoot, she won't see you anyway. She sees the family every bit like she was right in the midst of 'em. Pour yourself another sherry; it gets better as she goes deeper."

"Shhh," Luke's companion responded, "she's starting up again."

"Yes, suh, dinners at this 'ole table were events of a lifetime. I think I'll just sit here and rest awhile. I ain't gettin' no real rest though 'cause it comes alive every time I sit in this dinin' room. I see, hear and feel 'em. I can even smell the rosemary left on the plate beside the roast lamb. I hear the laughter, and I can see the silent tears."

"Didn't I hear Mr. Washington say somethin' about the Independence Day Celebration comin' up?" Papa asked. "I hope he don't plan on havin' any of that 540-acre property be ruined by those hooligans hollerin' about some freedom they ain't even got a real taste of yet."

That was Papa's way of changin' the subject. Cause Mama Tutu was just beginnin' to wash, dry and hang Huckabuck Marie's laundry in front of all the dinner guests. Papa looked up at me and nodded for some cream in his coffee. I rushed to pour it for him while Huckabuck Marie circled the table pourin' coffee with everyone's eye on her every move. Then Mama Tutu started up again.

"What's the matter with you chile, you scared to fill my cup up to the top?" she asked.

"I reckon she is leavin' room for 'da milk," I answered.

"Ain't nobody ask you nutin'," Mama Tutu said.

"Yes'm," was all I said after that.

Chapter XI

Church Community

Granville Independence Day celebration was just around the corner. The town was already full of visitors, and as usual Papa's home was a hub of activity. This year's celebration would be the biggest ever. It was 1890, ten years before the turn of the century. Mr. Washington was hard pressed travelin' all over the Union and Europe to drum up support for his ever expandin' industrial-agricultural institution. We needed scholarship funds. Most of the students were from families who could not afford the cost of the education or the supplies needed to pursue the course of study at the normal school. The church took the lead in organizin' events to build up the scholarship fund. The Board of Trustees decided that as long as you came to church, you could get a scholarship. Many of the children of the freed slaves had no family resources to depend on for educational fees. For many, it was only the family's faith that sustained them. Blindly believin' in the grace of God and the goodness of His people, they leaned on the church and made sure their children were faithful followers.

I had graduated with honors by then and had persuaded my family to sponsor two Granville youth at the Normal School with the money I earned workin' as Mr. Washington's assistant. I was also lookin' forward to the enrollment of my only little brother, Lil' Luke. Several Granville youth, includin' Lil' Luke, were helpin' the older students from the Normal School to set up booths along the parade route a couple of miles from what had come to be known as the Outlaw mansion. Lil' Luke was usually the first volunteer to arrive in the mornin' for his assignment.

The older students were given the task of transportin' the supplies and the samples from the school to the booths. I remember it was Lil' Luke's job to fill all the bottles up with cherry lemonade before settin' them out. The deacons who built the booths made them Lil' Luke's height so he could line up the bottles on the display. Mama Tutu made two barrels of the lemonade usin' lemons and cherries from her own orchard. The booths were covered with brightly yellow striped canvass to add an accent of color and to provide shade from the hot July sun. Lil' Luke was busy fillin' bottles before the men were finished constructin' the overhead canvass for the booth. He was remarkably efficient for his age. I remember watchin' him methodically stick each cork into the mouth at the top of each bottle and slap it on the head with his open palm to secure it in the bottleneck. After he had filled a dozen or so of these bottles of lemonade, he would stop for a moment and stack them carefully in the crates of dry ice on the table. He worked six hours out in the hot sun. By high noon, the lemonade was sellin' like hot cakes. Lil' Luke continued to keep the table stocked and the hotter it got the faster the stack went down.

He liked that job because he had a front line view of all the acts in the parade. There was the baton squad and the clowns in the front lineup followed by the pipes and drums. The biggest surprise though was the circus elephant that had been arranged by Mr. Washington. It was transported to Granville as a gift from one of his northern politician friends. In exchange, Mr. Washington had promised to give a speech at a political rally in the fall of that year. When Mr. Washington himself marched proudly past Lil' Luke's display booth, Lil' Luke held one of the lemonade bottles up as a salute to him. As he passed, Mr. Washington took off his hat and waved toward the stand. At the same time the announcer was announcin' him as the head master of the Normal School. As the announcer named some of his contributions, he mentioned the bottle invention and encouraged the crowd to make sure and purchase a bottled drink. The crowd cheered. I chuckled when Lil' Luke bowed as though they were cheerin' for him.

The parade went on until around 4:00 P.M. Lil' Luke helped pack all the display items into cedar boxes. He was anxious to get back home because he knew Huckaback Marie and Mr. Washington would all be joinin' our family for dinner after the parade. He saved the last two bottles of lemonade for us. It was his gift to me for my help in gettin' him the job at the stand.

Meanwhile, it had just started rainin'. Little drops tapped gently on the top of the canvass tent. Once the boxes were loaded onto the wheel barrel, one of the older students rolled it away. The endin' of the parade and the dismantlin' of the stands seemed a signal to the clouds that they were free to open up. With one blast of lightnin' followed by a rollin' thunder; the clouds parted and the rain poured. Lil' Luke had started down the road toward home when another cracklin' thunder-roll unleashed continuous sheets of staggerin' rain. He took off runnin' down the stretch of the windin' red clay road directly in front of our big porch. Once he could see the lights of the house in the distance, like a racehorse in the last mile of the race, he ran even faster. One of the older boys caught a glimpse of him from the balcony and said he looked like he was goin' as fast as lightin'.

Joy and laughter bounced from room to room like crickets at a barn dance that night at papa's house. Men, women and children were celebratin' their independence in the most elegant fashion affordable anywhere in the Union. The parade of food and cheer was endless. I noticed that Lil' Luke was not yet back home so I decided to take a walk outdoors to look after him. The harsh rain did nothin' to dampen my spirit so I grabbed the parasol hangin' from the huge dressin' bench sittin' in the vestibule. I stopped for a moment in front of the tall walnut-encased mirror to admire the lovely bright gingham dress Mama Tutu had created with its lace-bordered ruffles. It was a masterpiece deservin' of this festive occasion. The parasol was designed from the same fabric as my dress and added the class and distinction that only Mama Tutu could create.

I stopped to notice the plants on the porch and it was wonderful to see them gettin' drenched. This downpour was exactly what they needed. I opened my parasol and leaned out over the railin' to see if I could see Lil' Luke approachin' the house. I couldn't see him from the porch so I decided to walk down to the bend in the road and meet him there. The pourin' rain blurred my vision. As I rounded the bend, I could barely make out what seemed like somethin' flyin' toward me. I thought it was a nanny goat runnin' for shelter from the rain. Within seconds coursin' through the storm, I could see that it was a person.

The earth had been parched from the drought and was hard. Instead of soakin' into the ground, the rain formed sediment on the top of the road, makin' the surface slippery. Lil' Luke would've taken off his shoes, but he had his Mama Tutu's words planted in his brain: "Ain't no civilized Black eva' gonna be seen outdoors without his shoes." So he kept runnin', with his shoes on his feet. Between the slippery red clay and the leather on the soles of his shoes, Lil' Luke lost his footin' and tried to stop. Instead of stoppin', his feet went airborne. In a matter of seconds, I saw him fall backward and hit his back against the wet hard ground. His hands flung from side to side and both bottles went crashin' into the road. I dropped the parasol and started runnin'. I could see his motionless body in the distance lyin' on the road. When I reached him, his right wrist was cut at a vein and he was bleedin'. The fall onto his back had knocked all the wind out of him, and he laid there passive with blood minglin' in the red clay of the road's surface. Rain covered him like a shroud over his motionless body. As I got closer I noticed the pool of blood hardly distinguishable from the clay.

"Lil' Luke, Lil' Luke!" I shouted. I fell to my knees and saw the flow of his blood slowin' down as it dripped onto the soil. With the urgency and precision of an emergency medic, immediately I bent over him to administer mouth-to-mouth resuscitation. It was difficult to peel the broken bottleneck from his hand. Brushin' the glass away with my skirt, I grabbed his arm to feel for a pulse. I ripped a piece of the hem of my dress and wrapped it tight around his forearm to cut off any more loss of blood, somethin' I learned from Mama Tutu tellin' me stories about the cobwebs that old slave wives used in order to stop the bleedin' when their husbands' skin had been whipped open. Yet there was no trace of spiders under the wide open sky, no ceilin' beams or cobwebs, only dark clouds cryin' down upon us both. I saw his blood drippin', yet not pulsatin' from his vein like it should. I couldn't tell how much blood he had lost because by the time I got there the rain had washed away most of the blood that had gushed from his wrist.

Damn rain, damn rain! When we needed it, it didn't come. Rain don't know no difference 'tween flowers and poison berries. It was comin' down so hard I couldn't see what I was doin'. There was no response from anythin' I did. I held him in my arms and over my sobs I yelled.

"Help! Somebody, help!"

I knew nobody heard my cry over the loud talkin' and laughin' back at the house. Then the sky bursts open and the cruel rain poured down on us both. I tried desperately to revive him, but it was too late. How could this happen to such an energetic and vibrant young man? His blood drained from under the makeshift tourniquet while my body filled with rage. Yet it didn't matter what I felt because it didn't make it change. This cannot be happenin'. Any time Lil' Luke got in trouble; I could always get him out. Each time I knew just what to do, or what to say and he'd be smilin' again. I looked down at his leaden face, heard the sound of his final breath, and then he was gone. I watched him be gone right in the prime of his joy. He was gone, with his whole life before him. He was gone in the spring of his blossomin' manhood. All I could do was hold his wrist against my bosom and scream.

"No! No! No…"

It took months to recover from the death of Lil' Luke. If it weren't for the daily visits of Huckabuck Marie, I would have just wanted to die myself. Huckabuck Marie visited with me every day for weeks after that day. I couldn't accept the thought of not havin' Lil' Luke. I grieved until I couldn't grieve any more. Sometimes I woke up in the middle of the night hearin' him call me, "Pan Zee!"

"Is that you Lil' Luke?" I would ask.

Papa adopted another boy, Lil' Luke's age, and called him Luke too.

When we got the new Luke, one of the church deaconesses, who was always mindin' our business more than she minded her own, whispered over to Papa one day in church. "Thought it might help keep 'yo other chile from goin' banana south on you. Don't let his high yella complexion scare you. His mother was the white one, so he free."

Much as Papa did for his people, he wouldn't adopt no slave child. He used to always say slave children couldn't forget bein' slaves. "They won't shake it for the life of them," he said. He told us to watch them and see that they would always look for another master to be a slave again, and he wouldn't waste education, time and money on no slave. His children were free and they were gonna to be free forever.

"As long as he's free, I'll give him a go," said Papa.

The boy was too old to be adopted by a regular family. After prayer covenant group, in the preceding weeks, the news of Little Luke's death was buzzin' in the ears of every congregate. It never ceased to amaze me how prayer works. The churchwomen made all the arrangements for his funeral. As far as I was concerned the churchwomen had a little too much to do with our life. I wished Mama Tutu would stop havin' those prayer meetin's. Things that were personal got put to the public like it was an order from God himself. And the help poured in from poor innocent believers. God had a search and seize committee and the prayer group members were appointed to the tasks that were announced in prayer meetin's. Once the holy rollers got hold of a problem, any chance of fixin' it in the privacy of your own family was gone.

Such was the life in the church. Elder women, who shout and then faint, curiously reveal the mysteries of the gospel to little girls who sit and stare. With their braids lined in tight rows of hair as they stretched their necks to get a glimpse of what was happenin'.

"Turn around chile, pay attention, b'fo you get slapped."

It didn't seem safe in church to me at all. Those warnin's were serious and a corrective slap could come from anybody. And then we'd get another slappin' again by one of our kin for gettin' slapped in the first place.

How do you make any sense out of someone slain in the spirit to a ten-year-old? They would look back and stare in horror, fearin' the worse had af-flicted the person and hopin' with all their might that it wouldn't hit them. Then when the altar call comes you better not move. Don't matter at all that you can hardly hold your pee. This ain't the time to go. Anyone moves then will be baptized next Sunday 'cause all the churchwomen around you will take any movement as a sign that you want to go up. And any one of six sisters will grab you and your mama and walk you down the aisle. So you thank God for the layers of crinoline between you and the seat. You squeeze your legs tight together. You cannot rock from side to side. You are allowed to do nothin'. Just hold on as much you can 'til it's over. Before you know it, you gonna get pinched on the cheek.

"Aren't you dressed so nice today, sweetie," some church sister would say.

Right then you can feel the trickle come. Finally it's over, and you grin, curtsey, then rush out to meet all your friends waitin' out front as others are lined up for the outhouse.

"I'm first," one would scream.

"No you're not, I was out here before you," another would yell.

This meant absolutely nothin' to us kids. We never used the outhouse anyway. Like a swarm from a beehive, we zoomed to the rear of the church for a piss. All lined up with the wall shieldin' us from the rear, our arms full of ruffles while our eyes glistened with laughter to the point of tears.

There is one thing that bothered me so much about the churchwomen. You couldn't be just Pansy Outlaw and have a mother and a father. No. You were part of the whole family in the church. Every mother was your mother and every father was your father. In other words, there were no secrets. The prayer meetin' was the fastest way for a secret to get out, especially the ones you really didn't want to share.

One night one of the sisters was praisin' de Lawd for her sons. She was thankin' God that they would be comin' home and vowed to bring them into the house of 'de Lawd if 'de Lawd see fit to bring them home safely. Six of her boys had been fightin' with the northern battalion. Every one of them was still alive and the Yankee army was sendin' them back with a big pension for each one. You could see the woman was beside herself with joy and thanksgivin' for the return of her sons. But little did she know that she wasn't alone.

The Sunday them boys arrived at church there were fifteen to twenty sisters of Zion waitin' in the church lobby! I mean they was primped up with the best finery money could buy. They stood out there waitin', smellin' pretty, and flappin' their eyes like they lashes was goin' to propel them into paradise.

Huckabuck Marie and I heard them talkin' about the men comin' to town. That day we pretended we were lookin' for a bracelet I had dropped in the vestry on my way into church. Every single one of them had one thing on their mind. They milled around in the church lobby all dressed up in their best garments. Like leopards in the wild, they waited to pounce on their prey. Each one distinctly costumed in colors that highlighted the various tones of their skins so carefully adorned with exquisite accessories. Standin' together they formed a rainbow of beauty with one seamless thought that united them all. Their eyes twinkled with anticipation.

I really envied the simplicity of their dreams. Mine were much more complicated. Huckabuck Marie and I listened to their talkin'.

"What you think about livin' in Virginia?"

"Don't much matter to me, long as I'm livin' off that big pension!" said the lady in the orange hat.

"Don't bother your pretty little head about that 'cause you won't be goin'," replied the one in the pink skirt.

"Says who?"

"Says the one who got a letter," replied Clara Brown.

"Ugh!" chimed in the whole group.

"You didn't get no such thing," said another one of the ladies.

"Just because somebody got a letter doesn't mean anythin' anyway," claimed yet another.

"Everyone knows how lonely men get when they in the army. They'll send letters to anyone breathin', who can read," the lady in the orange hat said, and the crowd burst out laughin'.

Most of them started snickerin' to each other after that until one of them spoke over the laughter.

"I know the way to catch a man and readin', writin', or arithmetic won't help!" proclaimed Sara Brown.

They all laughed out loud until one of the older church sisters scolded them.

"Hush up, shhhhh! Can't you see we have company?" She was referrin' to Huckabuck Marie and me.

"No, don't hush up, they need to hear. Besides, you won't get no educated man that way," the orange hat lady quipped.

"I bet you one thing. You might not get 'em but you sure as hell gonna keep him that way," retorted one of the others.

"Lord have mercy, chile', you in God's house!" exclaimed another.

With all their meddlin', most of the time the churchwomen did help. In fact, for them to take such care to arrange everythin' for the adoption of the new Luke was compassionate and kind but it never was the same, especially not in the beginnin'. At first I got very angry about the nerve of them tryin' to replace Lil' Luke. It took me a while to accept the loss. It was important for me to grieve hard and seriously over the loss. I wanted to sit with the sadness for a little while. They acted too quickly to my likin', but the churchwomen were always swift with the cure. Huckabuck Marie continued her visits daily. With her encouragement, I came to love the new Luke, and since that time no one ever tried to explain any of it to him. They were like that, the Outlaws. They just kept goin' forward. Soon it was tucked away in the past and now it lasts only in my memory. I eventually had to let it be and it was largely because of Huckabuck Marie. She was just that kind of friend. She would come around and start tellin' me about all her troubles. She could bother herself about so many unimportant things that soon you would forget what was worryin' you. Each day that she came she had some ridiculous fret about herself, and within minutes I would be completely entangled in curlin' irons, petticoat lace, mud facials, or any such trifle.

It was a sunny day in March. She and I were sittin' on the front porch. I had just finished trimmin' my plants. They had grown up to the window and a few of them had already been transferred into a garden which was our secret memory of Lil' Luke. I used many of those experiments on my plants as part of my classroom instruction at the normal school where I taught. Strangely, I wasn't much older than some of the students. They were eager to learn, so they didn't mind and most of them were boys. There wasn't a whole lot of time left for girly things. Oh don't take me wrong, I liked teachin' boys, yet it left me longin' for the opportunity to just be a girl. With all the paperwork, I had very little time to pay attention to my own self.

I noticed that Huckabuck Marie, however, never loss even one eyelash without frettin' for days over it. When she wasn't fixin' her hair, she was pattin' powder on her face and paintin' her lips with rouge. Whatever it was about bein' a girl that I had sacrificed for teachin', I readily admit that Huckabuck Marie had enough of it for the two of us. I really appreciated her comin' to visit so regularly while I recovered from the tragedy but I really had no idea nor could I understand what was so important about whether your skin was dry or oily. As for hair, mine was so long that all I could do with it was to braid it and think of it as a sort of tail.

When Huckabuck Marie was not completely occupied with fussin' about herself. she would point out details about the few women that were in the school. My curiosity was sparked by a comment she made about Mr. Washington's missus. This was somethin' that she had pointed out earlier in the day when we were both still at the Normal School. I realized then that I was light years away from havin' a true sense of the importance of details regardin' face paint, coiffures, and all that stuff. I didn't understand, at all, how she could make news about lip paint sound like it had the importance of the birth of a colt.

"Did you ever notice that Missus Washington doesn't apply her lip paint until after she arrives?" asked Huckabuck Marie.

"Yes, and?" I wondered out loud.

What I wanted to know was what was it that made it so terribly significant about Missus Washington not applyin' her lip paint until after she arrived at the school office. So finally I asked, knowin' that Huckabuck Marie had meant to explain, entirely in detail, the whole thing and that's why she asked.

"So what's the big deal?" I asked.

She gave me a look like a wild fox starin' into a chicken coup. I had the feelin' I was goin' to loose somethin' right away, like maybe my innocence.

"Really, Pansy Outlaw, you would think a woman who could create a whole new method of plant fertilization would understand some of the simpler things in life also," she replied.

Immediately, I got uncomfortable. I wanted to withdraw my question. It revealed a level of ignorance that was embarrassin'.

"Oh yeah, I know why—sure," I said and then laughed.

"Sure what, Pansy Outlaw?" she asked back at me. "Don't think you are goin' to get away with that kind of answer."

"Well sure, I mean sure, because...well..." I fumbled for words.

"I knew it. You don't have the slightest idea why that is so important, do you?" she asked tauntingly.

"Well, I could guess." I replied.

We both laughed. Mine was a nervous laughter and she squealed like a duck.

"I see it's time to talk about the birds and the bees," she said with a big grin.

"Hey, now that's a subject that I can handle, " I replied, snippin' away at my plant siblin's. "I can tell you lots about bee hives, and I betcha' I can recognize every bird that lives within the state of Alabama. But Huck, what's that got to do with why Missus Washington came in to the school office without her lip paint on her mouth?" I asked innocently.

Huckabuck Marie laughed out loud again.

"Not those kinds of birds and bees," she said. "Sit down, Pansy," she continued with a gentle smile. "Let me start from the very beginnin'."

After that talk, I realized a true friendship had started. Mama never took the time to explain things like that. I was amazed at how much Huckabuck Marie knew and the number of highly respectable gents who, she recounted; she had to continually fend off. Many of the righteous had come beggin' her favor.

"Missus Washington was pleasin' her man, chile, and that's how a woman keeps her man interested," she stated.

"Why you think God created Eve?" she asked.

Then she answered the question for me.

"He wanted to give the man a little temptin'!"

I begin to relate to her sense of good and evil.

"The good Book makes it clear," she said.

"Keep your hands off somebody else's wife. A man's wife is fair game," she said.

Her strangely diluted version of a sermon suited me more than the long drawn out soliloquy on Sunday mornin'.

"You want to know why a town full of church goers would have a problem if they weren't fakin' livin' by the Good Book?" she asked. "'Cause if you can have the milk without buyin' the cow, why not drink all the milk you can get?" she answered herself.

"And that, my dear Pansy, is all you need to know about the birds and the bees."

Needless to say, I was in awe of her. I who had all the education there was to obtain was made speechless with one little story. So I sought her advice constantly on matters of that nature. I finally even convinced her to go with me to church on Sunday mornin's. At first she didn't agree to go. I'm not sure exactly what changed her mind but one thing I know for sure, when she did decide to go, I never before got that much attention at church.

That day she confided in me about her church experience.

"You see, Pansy," she said, "the church I grew up in kept God way above the congregation."

She told me how she was always starin' at the gold doors that shined from way up high in the middle of the altar. She believed that God was sittin' behind those doors. She always wondered, was he on a throne, hangin' on a cross like he was in the statues, or what? Maybe the scene behind the doors was God standin' in front of the tomb where he rose up from the dead, I thought. Huckabuck Marie told me that for her everythin' about God was hard to get to. He bein' so far removed, it made her have to pray especially hard to get God's attention.

In the Outlaw family church, you get God laid out in front of you. And who lays him out? Sometimes the biggest sinner hisself is the very one givin' you the holy baloney. You gotta watch what they's doin' and see if they sayin' the same thing. You still ain't gonna know much about God. All you really learn from them preachin' is either they is liars or they ain't. I tried to convince Huckabuck Marie to go with me. She said she would only do it to help me see the truth. One day she finally said yes.

"I'll go 'cause I want you to know who's sellin' the cheese, but don't expect me to change my personal beliefs for any of them sorry saints," she said.

"I'll just pretend you're my guardian angel," I replied.

"Hmph! I ain't never said I was no angel," she responded.

We laughed 'til our sides hurt. The rest of the afternoon, Huckabuck Marie gave my ears a full supply of ammunition for the world of 'holier than thou.' She had more enemies than peanuts on 'ole man Carver's farm, and most of them were at the church. When she finally did go, some of the deacons were very uncomfortable with her around.

She told me that when she turns down dey propositions, that's when the men make up stories and start to spreadin' around things they wish they had a chance to do with her, just for spite. People who she'd never even seen she'd be accused of doin' things with them.

I was beginnin' to see the light. Suddenly the chokin' protection from Papa and the careful guardin' of Mama Tutu began to make sense.

Huckabuck Marie admitted she was no angel, but if mercy was for sale at that church, you couldn't feed a church mouse with the profit. She didn't mind goin' with me, if I didn't mind goin' with her. She warned me that if I was goin' to be "somebody," she didn't want me to be known as "the friend of that hussy"—even though, I don't believe there was ever a more virtuous woman sittin' front row and down center before the admonishin' crowd.

"I could care less," I said. "Besides it takes more courage to be you and go there than to be them, sittin' there posin' for good." Huckabuck Marie promised me that if I ev'a called on da Lawd to cover up my shame, she would walk, leavin' me, the church, and the whole congregation. We agreed that whatever happened between us, we'd keep the faith. We vowed to never lose faith in ourselves, in each other, and in whatever sat behind those golden doors way up high that cannot be seen or heard.

"Do you promise?" I asked. She agreed and we shook on it.

Chapter XII

A Free Man

Slavery had left so many women single in the South that righteousness had taken a long hot summer vacation from church. Granville gossip was at a premium among the married. Most of the single women in town were after Mr. Washington. It didn't even matter that he was married. The women who once had husbands thought they were the only ones who knew how to handle him. They weren't lookin' for husbands so he, bein' married, was that much more attractive. Not that Mr. Washington needed any more qualities to make him attractive. His manner alone caused women to swoon.

Huckabuck Marie was just about the only woman in town that was not chasin' Mr. Washington. Once she got to know the missus, he automatically became an untouchable to her. She had a sense of loyalty about friendship that was uncommon to many of her peers. At a time when the competitive spirit had overcome most ambitious Southerners, she remained calm and reticent toward other women's husbands in general. If she ev'a got to know the wife, it would be strictly against her code of ethics to even as much as smile menacingly toward the husband.

It was this quality that Mr. Washington most admired in Huckabuck Marie. It earned her his trust and his confidence. That's how I knew all about the other women who were beatin' down the Normal School doors pretendin' they were interested in education. Huckabuck Marie had been summoned a many a day to escort dozens of such women out of the interview room. Each one lookin' more distraught than the other over their futile attempts to succeed in temptin' the headmaster into a dangerous liaison.

On one such occasion, Huckabuck Marie had returned to the Normal School after her midday walk to the post office where she went to retrieve the day's mail. She had been the one who set up this particular appointment earlier in the week, so it did not surprise her when the genteel widow arrived promptly. Actually it was more than prompt; she arrived a whole hour early for her appointment, so Huckabuck Marie decided to take a break. The next appointment wasn't for two hours, which would give her plenty of time to fetch the mail. She had the interview timin' down to a science, and once Mr. Washington had closed the door behind his guest it was guaranteed to take at least one hour before the entire interview was completed. In the meantime, she could make the trip to and from the post office. Everythin' went smooth durin' the introduction and things seemed pretty customary so once she saw the door close; she stepped out without any mention to the headmaster. The tale of that day became my second chapter in the birds and bees lessons. Huckabuck Marie explained to me that this sort of thing goes on all the time, but this time it nearly cost her job at the Normal school.

Mr. Washington has never forgiven Huckabuck Marie for leavin' him alone for that infamous appointment. His wife, who was also his administrative assistant, had gone to Virginia for a day trip to visit with her relatives and that left Mr. Washington alone with the widow in his office in the main buildin' of the school. The way I heard it, students were goin' about their routine chores while other classes were in session. Loud noises from the work that was bein' done by students layin' bricks banged over any other sounds. The student builders were layin' the foundation for another new buildin' and the resonant voices of the instructors echoed throughout the stately halls. Mr. Washington told us that he walked over to look at the work goin' on outside, and when he returned to talk he closed the window.

"That should make it better," he said.

As Mr. Washington described it, the interview started with the simple format that was used for all perspective students. Huckabuck Marie retold the story many times with dozens of variations, but the first time she told it to me she told it exactly as it had been told to her.

For every question that Mr. Washington asked the widow, she would respond with a question for him.

"So, ma'am, what is it that you wish to learn here at the Normal School?" asked Mr. Washington?

"I am terribly fond of cigars, Mr. Washington. How about you—do you smoke?"

"No ma'am, I don't, well...on some occasions, I suppose, I have enjoyed some of the finest tobacco grown. My favorite tobacco is home grown and individually wrapped in Cuba," he answered.

Realizin' he had drifted from the subject of the interview, he ventured to bring the conversation back to questions regardin' her pursuit of education.

"Uh-huh, so, you want to learn how to grow tobacco?"

"No, suh, I already knows how to grow that. The 'ole rascal I was married to loved him some tobacco, so I learned myself how to grow it. Still have a fresh patch growin' in my kitchen garden. Would you like some? I mean, for some special occasion?" she asked.

"No, thanks just the same," he said.

"So have you brought your letter of recommendation with you today?" asked Mr. Washington.

It was an awkward attempt to steer the interview again back to the purpose of the meetin'.

"Oh sho', I got it tucked away safely. I suppose you want to see it, don't you?" she offered.

She started takin' up her dress and then her petticoat.

"Well, we can get to that letter, I mean, later," he interrupted.

Huckabuck Marie said he broke out in a sweat just tellin' this part.

She let the dress fall down but then quickly reached down inside the front of her dress where lace smockin' crossed her chest and pulled out a cigar.

"I almost forgot, I did bring you a present from my garden."

She started toward him with the cigar stretched out from the tip of her lacey covered fingers. He reached way out in front of himself to take it so that she could begin to retreat. Instead she kept comin' toward him.

"I'm much obliged," he said and went to sit down at his desk so he could put it in his cigar box. He reached above the desk to open the rollaway cabinet where he kept it. Before he knew it, that widow leaped right onto his lap like a long-legged kangaroo from hell. She wrapped her legs around him sayin', "Take me now, suh, take me now."

Huckabuck Marie was fallin' out laughin' at this part of the story. She said it was even funnier when Mr. Washington was tellin' it to her. He explained that he did all that he could do to keep from fallin' onto the floor carryin' the widow down on top of him. He stood up and walked to the door with the widow draped around his waist. He then opened the office door and walked down the hall to the front entrance with her steadily climbin' all over him and beggin' him to have his way. There wasn't a soul in the hallway to cause her any restraint. She just hung on, kickin' and screamin' for mercy.

"Have mercy on my poor soul, massa. I do anythin' for one kiss, just one," she begged.

She kept tryin' to put her mouth on his while he twisted and turned to avoid her lips. Whatever got into that 'ole widow, Mr. Washington neva' did figure out. Now Mr. Washington was no religious man, but Huckabuck Marie said she knew one thing that day had given him a sudden appreciation for the term "up jumped the devil."

He was very careful from that day on to avoid un-chaperoned interviews with 'ole widows. Huckabuck Marie or his missus was always within earshot of the room whenever he interviewed any single woman. When he felt like he was gettin' into a tight spot with one of the women he would simply cough or clear his throat and either his secretary or his wife would knock on the door and request his attention for some fictitious detail.

Mr. Washington was terribly close to his third wife, and Huckabuck Marie realized this from watchin' them work together. There was nothin' he didn't share with her. She was the companion of his thoughts, the inspiration for his actions, and the benefactor of his deeds. Should there be any exception to this bond of trust between he and his wife, it was either with me or Huckabuck Marie. We were the only other people beside her in Granville he trusted, and we were considered next of kin for his shared confidences.

I didn't know, and neither did Huckabuck Marie understand, exactly what it was about us that made him hold us so close to his inner sphere of trust. One thing we did both know was that it was his magnificent spirit that held us to him and inspired us to serve him. What we just couldn't imagine was what it was that held him to us. Huckabuck Marie had started workin' when the school opened just as Mr. Washington had promised her. He believed in my ability to study science and never once questioned why I was interested in it. His word was always the only contract that was ever necessary to close a deal. Before I even sent General Armstrong my application to the normal school, Mr. Washington had already decided I was goin' to enter his program. He said he was convinced by my own testimony and love for science more than any letters of recommendation. Huckabuck Marie was the only other person who knew about it. I had to tell somebody. I had grown entirely too big for the secret tree top journalin', and so the three of us grew into a pyramid of power.

Within the same year of my graduation from the normal school, I was appointed as instructor. Hence, I became the very first female instructional assistant for academic studies. I cherished this position almost as much as I cherished him. I was teachin' school from the time I was sixteen. Numerous times durin' the nine years at the Normal School Mr. Washington defended my position, before the Board, against attacks by the male instructors and quieted complaints by jealous students.

"Your dreams are my dreams," he would say. He fully supported us through opportunities at the school and in our personal endeavors and goals.

One night Huckabuck Marie had stopped by the saloon on her way home from the school office. Although she had a respectable new career at the Normal School and had tempered the rough talk and discouraged all those unwanted advances, still in some quarters of town she had not quite outlived her reputation. It didn't matter that the nasty rumors were entirely based on hearsay and empty gossip; there were certain things about her that made that reputation stick. Her fondness for the saloon crowd was one of those things. I know that any time before nine o'clock in the evenin' is considered early at the saloon. When Huckabuck walked in, it was barely past seven. She always received a hearty welcome because she was one of the few town people with a steady job and a generous streak when it came to toastin' the house at her expense. It was on a day when she and the other workers had just received a bonus from the sale of a shipment of bricks manufactured at the Normal School. The crowd at the saloon was still sparse so she ordered a round for everyone. They were all leanin' on the counter like washed out potato sacks hangin' on a rail to dry.

"Doc, let 'em roll, eva'body's comin' up winners tonight."

"Okay, Miss Huck, you call 'em, I toss 'em!"

Cheers rolled down the bar and applause filled the room. Huckabuck Marie made her way through those gathered at the bar after greetin' some folks she hadn't seen for a while and then sat down in her favorite booth in the far corner of the saloon. I heard she knew everyone in the place but the fella who was sittin' at the piano. After she tossed down a shot of whisky, she yelled over to him from her seat in the corner.

"Hey, stranger, you just takin' up space at that piano stool, or are you gonna play us a tune?"

"What's it to you, lady? Why don't you come over here and give me some inspiration," answered the man.

"Did you hear that, Doc? The man needs inspiration. You betta' roll 'em again and give the piano player a double," she ordered.

"All round and one double on the roll," replied Doc Holiday, the bartender.

The stranger at the piano poked out a few unrecognizable notes and the crowd started booin'.

"Hey, Huck," one of the other men shouted, "Your piano man should try whistlin' Dixie, cause his playin' is far from entertainin'."

"Oh, give him a chance, boys," she yelled, "maybe he needs someone to push the pedals."

Huckabuck Marie got up and walked over to the piano stool and sat down beside the man. She motioned to Doc to fill him up again and called for a toast.

"Let's toast to the piano duo!"

The rest of the men hollered, "Here, here!"

Huckabuck Marie started pumpin' the pedals and the stranger took one look over his shoulder at her and was overtaken by the whiskey's effect. Once he got sight of her allurin' taffeta bodice, he automatically reached for her and his hand fell right into the valley of her voluptuous bosom. Huckabuck Marie immediately jumped to attention and whirled around with the force of a hurricane, slappin' the dastardly fool so hard that he fell backward off of the piano stool. He crashed into one of the ladies that had come closer to hear him play. Seein' him fall on the lady, the chap who was standin' right next to her picked up the stranger and punched him so hard he slammed across the piano top. Needless to say, a riot broke out in the place. Chairs and tables were flyin' everywhere. Before the fightin' ended one man was dead and another customer was arrested for the killin'.

Before the week was over, Huckabuck Marie received an order from the sheriff to answer a charge of disorderly conduct.

"How can I be charged for defendin' myself?" she asked.

I wasn't about to argue that point. I just reminded her that a man was killed in a brawl after she slapped a drunk one night while visitin' the local saloon. It wouldn't have been beneath the sheriff to try to pin the whole thing on her.

"Do you need me to tell you how lucky you are,that you're not the one dead?" I asked.

"The worst thing you lookin' at is a temporary ban from the saloon and a nighttime curfew." I didn't see the harm either of those things could do her.

I promised to go to the sheriff's office with her, but I wasn't goin' to promise that there wouldn't be a consequence. If it hadn't been for Mr. Washington, things could have gotten way out of hand and she may have been given a jail sentence.

The next day I was waitin' for Jake to separate the sack of mail that I was pickin' up for Huckabuck Marie. She was takin' some time off at home awaitin' the hearin' date. Across the counter from where I was standin', was the sheriff's office with the door wide open. I overheard a conversation between him and the chief magistrate talkin' about the saloon incident.

"I think we should outlaw women entirely from the saloon," said the sheriff.

"We could create an ordinance forbiddin' women from enterin' a saloon unless they are escorted by their husbands, but I don't think we can ban them completely," responded the magistrate.

"Why not?" asked the sheriff.

"If it wasn't for that foolhardy Huckabuck Marie, none of this would have happened," continued the sheriff.

"Aren't you bein' just a little bit harsh on Miss Huckabuck Marie? From what I heard, she was merely defendin' her honor."

"She gonna be defendin' more than her honor. I'll see to it that she pays for the killin' personally."

I knew the sheriff was lookin' for a scapegoat. So I went hurriedly to Mr. Washington and sought his advice.

"You're right, Miss Pansy," Mr. Washington said, after hearin' about the conversation between the sheriff and the magistrate. "They 'gonna go after Huckabuck Marie."

"She's had it," I sighed, holdin' my head between the palms of my hands in dismay.

"You bring Missus Huckabuck Marie to the house tonight and I'll see what sense I can make of this mess."

"But she'll need someone to represent her," I said, "and not too many people in this town are goin' to go up against the sheriff and the magistrate, especially not for Huckabuck Marie."

"Too many people spoil the broth," smiled Mr. Washington. "Besides she'll have the two best people in town on her side, and that's you and me."

That night Mr. Washington, Huckabuck Marie, and I went over the whole incident forward and backward. Mr. Washington got names for witnesses and sketched out the scene that involved Huckabuck Marie. He compared where she was standin' to the position of the killin' and clearly demonstrated that the whole crowd stood between Huckabuck Marie and the man who got stabbed.

Mr. Washington went with us to the sheriff and presented a solid case in defense of Huckabuck Marie. To our amazement the charges against her were dropped. On the way back Mr. Washington asked Huckabuck Marie if she would like to stop at the saloon to celebrate. We all had a good laugh. That night Mr. Washington said that freedom had a price tag and "a sharp mind can clean up the damage of a quick fist faster than a blinkin' eye can miss a shootin' star!"

"One thing about bein' free," he said, "you gotta' learn how to defend your freedom by usin' your mind, or your freedom gonna' be the very thing send you straight to an early grave."

Chapter XIII

All the Tired Horses

Sunday was the day of rest. There was a promenade of carriages lined up around the circular driveway in front of the Colored Methodist Church of Granville. The ladies and the gentleman were fully dressed in their Sunday best outfits. Children were fidgetin' with the tucks and ties of their suits and dresses. After each family was assisted from their carriage and ushered into the crowded threshold of the sanctuary, the horses were led away by one of the church field hands. I used to get the jitters from sight of the field hands because I knew they were the same folks that dug the graves. Are you some kind of zombie if you spend your whole life diggin' graves? It was always hard for them to get the horses to settle. Looks like the horses could sense somethin' strange about them too. After a struggle, each horse drawn coach was lined up in front of the fence on the inside of the church cemetery. And sometimes they led the horses out to pasture while services were bein' held but only if they weren't busy diggin' some poor souls hole in the ground.

"Mornin', Rev," greeted Mama Tutu who was usually one of the early arrivals.

"Mighty fine day in de Lawd," said the Right Reverend Daniel L. Pickett, standin' at the threshold of the church to greet his parishioners.

Every Sunday I made a first stop at the cemetery where I would place a fresh bouquet of handpicked flowers from my garden at the headstone of my beloved real brother, Lil' Luke. That Sunday was special because it was the day we would have been celebratin' his birthday. When I replaced the old flowers with the new ones, I sat down beside the gravestone. Tear drops moistened the skirt of my dress as the pain of his death seared through my heart again. I knew then that it would never stop hurtin'. Holdin' back my head, I looked up into the sky and remembered the sound of his youthful voice.

"Pan Zee, why is the sky blue?" was one of his favorite questions.

I just didn't have an appetite for hell, fire and damnation as I stared into the clear blue sky. I was so lost in the revelry of scenes with Lil' Luke.

Inside, the church choir had already finished two rousin' praise songs which were so loud I could hear them from the cemetery. I could just imagine the congregation tappin' and swayin' to the rhythm of the glory train.

"I'm goin' home on the mornin' train... the evenin' train may be too late... oh I'm goin' home on that mornin' train..." sang out the church peoples. Most of them had never been on a train so these songs gave them hope that someday they too would get on board the new transportation machine. The music lured me in and I stood in the doorway so I could take in the whole scene. The sunlight shined through the circular stained glass window below the church steeple. The fragments of fluorescent rays speckled over the faces of the jubilant assembly. It was time for the offertory prayer and the passin' of the baskets. The second collection was held to support the Normal School. Jasper Ale always made the invitation forceful and heavy laden with guilt.

"I know some of you had a hard year, crops suffered from the dry spell we had," he said.

"But 'da Lawd seed to it that ya had crops, Amen?" he continued.

"I believe 'ole Doc Holiday, back there," he said, pointin' to the rear of the one-room church, "can help me remember some of 'dem farmers that's been feelin' d'ere oats last Friday night, ain't that right, Doc?"

Doc Holiday shook his head affirmatively.

"But 'da Lawd know and we ain't castin' a single stone at any sinner today, Amen?"

"Now I know the Doc to be a reasonable man, so I'm for certain 'dat he know one tenth of the till he took in Friday, belongs to the Lawd, Amen. Can I get an Amen?"

"Amen," chanted the congregation in unison.

"I see the Outlaw family right ch'ere in de front row, as usual,' he continued.

"Oh, but wait a minute, Reverend, I don't think I see Miss Pansy," Jasper Ale touted. "Humph! Devil must be workin' the big tithers today," he teased. He walked down the stairs toward the deacon's bench still whispering under his breath yet loud enough for Mama Tutu to hear him.

"Seems nobody can control that youngin'," he said, glaring straight at Mama Tutu.

Mama Tutu's eyes bulged and she was about to lunge toward 'ole Jasper Ale. Instead he tripped over the edge of the altar railing and fell backward into his seat.

The startled congregation exhaled a loud harmonious ahhh at the near collapse of Jasper Ale.

Mama Tutu, ignoring 'ole Jasper Ale, directed her response to the pastor.

"She stopped by the cemetery, Reverend," she said defensively. "She'll be joinin' us in a minute."

Huckabuck Marie sat squirming in her seat right next to Mama Tutu. Usually Pansy sat there between her and Mama Tutu, neutralizing the angst Huckabuck Marie felt every time she was anywhere near Mama Tutu. Unfortunately that day there was nothing separating her from the electric panic that was coursing through her body. So she tried to disappear by slinkin' down in the pew. She knew dang well that if Pansy was missin', somehow it was going to be her fault. She grew more and more pale with fright as Mama Tutu turned toward her. Her mind took in the obtrusive pressure like a slow motion glimpse of a near fatal fall.

Huckabuck Marie looked down at her feet, scared to look up because she knew Mama Tutu's eyes cocked toward her, would demand to know the whereabouts of Pansy Outlaw. Which she usually knew, but that day she didn't have a clue.

"Where she at, chile?" asked Mama Tutu somewhat pleadingly.

Huckabuck Marie shrugged her shoulders and squeamishly looked sideways at Mama Tutu as if expecting a back handed slap. Instead, Mama Tutu just stiffened her back and faced forward.

I was still day dreamin' about Lil' Luke while all this was goin' on inside the church. So I slipped backward out of the door and returned to Lil' Luke's grave. I sat down leanin' my back against the headstone. Starin' up at the sun-drenched, peachy brown treetops against the powder blue skies made my heart fly into the open air. It was just too beautiful to be cooped up in church. I began to think more deeply of Lil' Luke, and the things he liked to do. That's when I bent over and whispered to the ground in the direction of his head.

"What do you want to do for your birthday, Lil' Luke?" I asked.

I listened for the answer and, from deep inside my heart, the answer came as clear as a bell. It came in a song we used to sing together.

"All the tired horses in the sun, how we goanna get any ridin' done."

It was his voice tellin' me that he wanted to go ridin' for his birthday. It was the perfect answer for my weary heart especially since I was the one who taught him how to ride. So I stood up and ran through the cemetery gate toward the field where the horses were restin'. I harnessed Bessie, the mare whose life I had saved, and stood a few feet from her side and with a runnin' start threw my body across Bessie's bare back. With one nudge of the heeled shoes I was wearin', we were off and runnin'.

I rode my guts out, over the hills and into the valleys of Granville's countryside. Bessie seemed delighted with this rump through the grassy fields. I stopped at the stream to let her get a drink and then she sprang across it. She was so excited that I had to pull back on the reins to keep her from splashing too much water on my Sunday dress.

It wasn't long before I heard the noon church bells ringin' in the distance. I knew the church service would soon be lettin' out. Fellowship might last another hour, and then the ushers would be goin' to the field to fetch the horses. I turned Bessie toward the sound of the bells and gave her a poke with both heels and she flew. When we reached the cemetery, they hadn't come for the horses yet so the gate was still latched. That's when I leaned back and sunk my heal into that mare's gut.

"This one's for you, Lil' Luke," I whispered, as I galloped toward the gate.

"Up, up and away!" With a slight tug on the rein, she took that gate like an angel in flight.

"D'ere you go, Luke, d'ere you go, baby brother!" I screamed in total ecstasy.

In the meantime, Huckabuck Marie was feverishly lookin' all over the grounds for me. I tied Bessie up and found her walkin' toward the front lawn. When she saw me, I was wobblin' a little on legs that hadn't used that much power for anythin' in a long time. She rushed over to see if I was hurt.

"Land sakes, Pansy, you look like you been through a cotton gin," she said and started pickin' grass off of my dress and shakin' her kerchief all over my body to dust me off.

"Where on earth have you been? I been worried sick about you!" she asked.

"I been havin' the best time in my life," I said. "Just me and Lil' Luke."

"Lil' Luke? Luke is in church with your momma and papa," she responded with surprise.

"No, the real Lil' Luke," I said.

"Oh, now I know you have gone plumb mad. Is it sun stroke?" she asked.

I decided to let that go. I wasn't in the mood for no arguin', and Huckabuck Marie and I could get into some serious arguin' if the time was right. I just laughed, and we tried to tidy up my dress for the ride home.

"Look at all those tired horses in the sun," I said, "and can't you see 'ole Bessie is ready and rarin' to go for another run!" I declared.

Now while I'm sittin' here in the reverie of yesteryear, and much as I love Luke III, I know he ain't no real Outlaw. I keep thinkin', if he knew his mama was a white woman, he might stop worryin' so much about bein' black. Well the truth is, he black all right but he ain't the real deal. The funny part is he don't know it, 'cause when our family takes in a chile that chile is ours. No need in tellin' him he ain't blue-blooded like the rest of us Outlaws. Sometimes I used to wonder how he be so smart and could get it all wrong and don't even know it. I only found out about his mama from Huckabuck Marie soon after we became close friends.

I remember the day she told me the whole truth. It was a beautiful day laced with sunshine just like the day I went ridin' on Lil' Luke's birthday. Fluffy white clouds were sailin' across the sky but it was a cold day. She was still workin' at the Stagecoach Junction then. One stagecoach left every mornin' and one arrived every afternoon. Just before Huckabuck found out about the general comin' to Granville, she witnessed the strangest departure from our town of one of the town folk that few if any people knew. I've asked her at least a thousand times to tell me the story, and each time I heard it, I wept again.

It was still early in the mornin' and the sun hadn't warmed up the air yet, so Huckabuck Marie threw a flint into the makeshift wood-burnin' pit at the edge of town where the coaches pulled out headin' north. A few arrived from the South bringin' injuns in search of work or a chance to seek refuge from the northern freeze. The mornin' stagecoach had already arrived and unloaded its passengers. The cowpoke that rode it in was off to the saloon for a refuelin' of whisky. He left the stagecoach beside the road and his passengers weren't scheduled to leave for another hour. This woman walked toward Huckabuck Marie and spoke very rough and unfriendly to her.

"Ain't d'ere no place to wait inside for the next stagecoach?" she asked.

"Sorry, ma'am. Some days if it wasn't for the wood burnin' in this pit over here, I'd freeze to death," Huckabuck Marie replied, "but you're welcome to join me."

The woman cautiously walked toward Huckabuck Marie, grumblin' about the cold.

"You wouldn't think it could be this bitter cold with the sun shinin' so damn bright," she said. The gruffness in her voice and manner was strange for a white gal which put Huckabuck Marie on notice and she stiffened up before respondin'.

"Oh! Mornin's are cold. That's why I dug this hole and am feedin' it dried tree limbs," Huckabuck Marie answered.

The woman slowly moved closer to the warmth of the fire. Huckabuck Marie then noticed her petticoat was hangin' below a frayed dress hem. The collar was crackin' at the creases, and she looked like she hadn't slept for days.

"Are you goin' on the stagecoach?" Huckabuck Marie asked.

"I am if the driver comes back before consumption gets me," she replied.

"Are you sick, ma'am?" Huckabuck Marie inquired.

"Yes, ma'am, I'm sick of this town, the people, and the goddamn massa," she answered angrily.

"Massa? What da' ya mean? You ain't got no massa and we free now. We ain't got no more massa. Not unless we want to," Huckabuck Marie said.

"You ain't never free from the man who raped you," the woman sharply responded. "And believe me it's double bad when a child comes out of it," she sat wringin' her hands as if they were knobs that could turn off the flow of her tears. "Then you hate the child too," she said, sobbin', "like he the one done that to you. So to make sure I don't have to look at that child no more, I'm leavin'."

"And what about the child?" asked Huckabuck Marie, ever so gently.

"He can rot in hell for all I care!" Now regainin' her composure, she continued, "All I know is they took him to the church, and what they did with him ain't no business of mine."

"And you, where will you go?" Huckabuck Marie inquired.

"I'll be gone, that's all I know," she said.

Huckabuck Marie felt so sorry for the woman. She convinced the woman to go with her into town until the stagecoach was ready to leave. All she had with her was her stagecoach ticket and a small sack containin' all her worldly possessions.

"Come on, chile, let's put out this fire and see if we can't burn off some of your troubles with a dose of Doc Holiday's tonic," Huckabuck Marie said.

The woman followed her into town, head hung with grief and draggin' her feet. Huckabuck Marie gave her some food and a little cash for the trip before they returned to the pickup spot. The tonic musta' got the woman talkin', and she told Huckabuck Marie the whole sad story about her tragic life and how her mama had left her with her nanny and she fell in love with her nanny's son. She layed with him at Massa's house and when the massa caught them she had to claim rape. The boy was hung and she couldn't bare to look at the child and so she ran away and gave him to the church.

"Tonic will tell on you," said Huckabuck Marie.

Many times I had asked Mama Tutu to tell me more about Luke III. She refused. Said if I knew too much I'd stop believin' in him. One day while Mama Tutu was busy makin' buns, I asked her where was Luke's inheritance. She sprinkled on the cinnamon and sugar and continued rollin' out the dough as though she didn't hear the question. Instead she responded with a question.

"See how easy it is to turn out a pan of sticky buns?" she asked.

Her sticky buns were so good. I've never been able to get them so chewy and soft. Every ingredient in perfect proportions packed with raisins and smothered in a sugary cinnamon glaze. If I knew what I know now, I should've been askin' for the recipe for them cinnamon buns and not about family history. But no, I kept pressin' for information about where Luke came from.

I can hear her words echo in my mind, "Land's sake, gal, why you always askin' about them outcasts?" she asked. "I know I taught you never to forget the past, but I didn't mean you was supposed to look back and stare," Mama Tutu advised.

"I thought his inheritance could pay for some of the expensive schoolin' Papa gave him," I told her.

She just said, "Never you mind."

Still I insisted.

"Lord have mercy, chile'. Why you keep tryin' to dig up his roots? Ain't no harm in Negroes learnin' about 'de history, but God help the fool that gets stuck in the past. What is it you wanna' know?" she asked.

"What does he have?" I asked.

"Purpose. He's got purpose." And that's all she would say.

"Purpose is the fruit of pain and joy is the product," Mama Tutu chimed. One day you'll see the joy part 'cause I'll fo' sure never live to see it."

It wasn't about his family's wealth that I wanted information. It was because I wanted to know what kind of woman would have the nerve to leave her baby. I don't think my own life would ever have had purpose without both Lukes. It's really strange that he still doesn't know about the white plantation slave owner that was his mother. I hope he never finds out. Let him just have the joy of bein' the first black legislator. I hope I live long enough to see that.

Chapter XIV

The Ride Home

After church was over every one filed out into the gardens while the field hands started linin' the buggies up in the driveway. Bessie was so jumpy that Papa could hardly keep the carriage still 'til Mama Tutu and the rest of the family climbed aboard.

"Whoa…Whoa. Now, girl, I don't know what's gotten into Bessie. Whoa—Whoa…Bessie!" yelled Papa Judd Outlaw, snatchin' back on the reins.

The ride home was rough. Papa had to hold tight on the reins the whole way. Bessie was chompin' at the bit. She had gotten the spirit and she couldn't stop tryin' to run away with it. Mama Tutu warned Papa, "If you can't control this feeble mare, I might have to take over drivin' this carriage."

Huckabuck Marie was busy chatterin' in the rear of the buggy criticizin' everythin' she could think of about me. She continued complainin' about my appearance and kept insistin' on me tellin' her where I had been while the service was goin' on and how I came to get so dusty.

"My dear, you even smell funny," Huckabuck Marie grumbled.

"Oh shush, Huck, will you please hush up," I said. I was the only one who could call her by the short version of her name without gettin', scolded 'bout the proper way of callin' her.

"Oh, sure, Pansy, you go missin' for three hours, come back dusty, sweaty, and smellin' like a stable boy, and I'm at fault for wantin' to know what is goin' on with you," she angrily replied.

"I'll tell you later. Now hush up, before Mama Tutu notices," I said.

Papa was finally able to keep the carriage runnin' smooth and Mama Tutu felt comfortable enough now to turn to the rear to address me.

"Miss Pansy!" she shouted.

"Yes, ma'am," I said meek and humble as I could.

"And where were you this mornin'?" she asked. "Do you know Reverend Pickett singled you out in front of 'da whole congregation, chile?"

"No, ma'am, I didn't know that," I replied tryin', to be calm and nonchalant.

"Well how could you know it? 'Cause you wan't d'ere!" she screamed.

"Yes'm," I said, then I turned to Huckabuck Marie and poked her.

"Say somethin'," I whispered.

"Uh...ummm...sure was some good singin' this mornin' wasn't it?"

"Yes, I d'clare it was," added Papa.

Mama, she just sat facin' the front with her pink parasol over her shoulder. She didn't say a word. She knew I was in for a scoldin' and she didn't want to add to it. I think her and Papa was both lookin' for a window of escape for me since they both knew what day it was and the deep sorrow that I was feelin'. It didn't faze Mama Tutu, however, who kept pesterin' me for answers.

"I'm warnin' you, Pansy Outlaw, I'm too 'ole for twistin' 'round the truth. I means to find out where you been. You musta' loss yo' las' mind if you think I'm 'goanna be a liar to 'de Reverend for you or any of you other Outlaws?" she said pointin' her finger around in a swoop.

"I be talkin' to you later, Miss Pansy," she said with her finger pointin' finally at me.

"Yes'm," I said, and not another word.

Huckabuck Marie and I looked at one another and kept quiet.

When Papa pulled the carriage up to the front porch, I was the first to jump down. Huckabuck Marie quickly followed me into the house. Papa helped Mama Tutu and Mama was still waitin' for help on her turn to step down. Instead Mama Tutu immediately got Papa's attention and the two of them started walkin' toward the house.

"I know you think I'm hard on Pansy, Judd, with today bein' Little Luke's birthday," Mama Tutu said. "You betta' set her straight before it's too late. You and I both know where she was durin' the sermon today, and she 'da one need salvation now, not Luke."

"Yes'm," Papa replied.

After Papa had assisted Mama Tutu safely to the porch, he turned to assist Mama down from the carriage. She was already walkin' toward the house; her face was stiff and emotionless. When it came to authority at the Outlaw house, it was Mama Tutu and not Mama who had the last word. She walked past Papa and irately made her way into the drawin' room.

Mama Tutu was sittin' in that same rickety rockin' chair that she had used so many times to rock the fears out of me. She sat there waitin' for me to come downstairs.

"Your chile don't need to go plum mad over somethin' that's in de Lawd's plan. I raised yuh wit de fear of God in yuh, and long as I got breath in my body me and my house will serve de Lawd," she announced to Judd Outlaw.

Judd Outlaw stood by the open hearth packin' his corn pipe with tobacco.

"Yes, ma'am, I always says what's good for the goose is good for the gander," he replied.

"E'va since de devil done practically took up residence here," she mumbled, (referrin' of course to Huckabuck Marie) "we in fo' hard times fo' sho'."

Papa knew better than to defend havin' Huckabuck Marie around. He perceived that comment as a pure trap so he found a polite way to exit.

"Now, if you'll excuse me, I'm fittin' to sit out on the porch and have a smoke."

"Go on," Mama Tutu said. "I'm gonna get to the bottom of this 'fo 'dem church folk come 'round here askin' 'bout 'dat chile of yawz."

Meanwhile, I was upstairs relivin' the events of the day with Huckabuck Marie.

"Huckabuck Marie! You just don't understand," I said. "I heard the voice of Little Luke."

"Oh Lawdy, chile, and you think yo' Mama Tutu is goin' to excuse you from church when you tell her that!" she yelled.

"I know it sounds strange, but it's the truth."

"Truth or no truth, you betta' think up somethin' else to tell 'ole battle-axe Tutu, or she'll swear haint got your soul," Huckabuck Marie bellowed with laughter.

"Huckabuck Marie, do you mean you don't believe me?" I asked.

"Okay, so you heard this voice. What did it say?"

"It said, 'All the tired horses in the sun, how we gonna get any ridin' done,' and it was Luke, honest it was him," I explained.

"And because he said this, you decided to skip worship and go ridin' off into the fields?"

"What would you do?" I asked.

"First of all I would have told him to hush up and then I would'a got my hind parts into the church as soon as possible!"

"Ugh. Lawd, chile, and I thought I could trust you to understand."

"Pansy! Pansy Outlaw! Come on down here, gal," Mama Tutu yelled up the stairs.

"Uh-oh, now what you gonna do?" Huckabuck Marie asked .

"I'll just tell her the truth. She won't believe no lie."

"In that case, I'll be goin'. I'll talk to you later, sweetie, 'cause she'll for sure blame this whole thing on me."

Both of us went down the stairs, I walked toward the drawin' room and Huckabuck Marie walked toward the door.

"Good day, ma'am," Huckabuck Marie said, "I sure enjoyed that singin' this mornin'. I look forward to joinin' y'all next Sunday. God bless your sweet soul. I sure loved that sermon too." Huckabuck Marie wiggled her fingers in the air to me and winked from behind the drawin' room door.

I looked back to get a last look of sympathy from Huckabuck Marie, but she was gone. I went over to sit next to Mama Tutu who listened intently to the whole story. When I had finished tellin' her, I was completely surprised at how she responded.

"Well. I knew close as you was to that boy that he would come to you some day," she said.

"You mean...you don't think I'm possessed by spirits?"

"Oh yeah, chile, you been possessed by a spirit all right, it just ain't a bad spirit. It's the spirit of our boy Lil' Luke. He done come to me a many a night. I guess he thought you wouldn't be able to handle it lessen' it was his birthday. He sho' tickle me, huh, huh, huh, huh, huh..." Mama Tutu's hearty laughter filled the house. "Lil' Luke still got a sense of humor, and he still got you, like putty, in the palm of his hands."

I sat there flabbergasted. Here I was a young woman, yet I was expectin' the worst beatin' of my life. Instead, I learned a little more about the way we believe. Somethin' happened that day that changed the way I saw the world and the way the world was gonna see me. Since Mama Tutu talked with spirits too, I must have her special gift, and that was all the proof I ever needed about that.

Chapter XV

The Zenith of His Fame

By late 1895, a flood of mail arrived every day at the Granville post office for Mr. Washington. After his electrifyin' speech at the Atlanta Exposition, he triggered an outpourin' of sentiment from all over the nation that fell on Granville, like a monsoon rain in August. We got so much mail that we had to open a mailroom at the school. I hired my cousin Josh, who was studyin' at the Normal School, to be our mailroom clerk. Mr. Washington had made sure that Josh got into the school and it was no doubt we needed the help. Accordin' to Huckabuck Marie that was about the same time that Mr. Washington's travel itinerary got very complicated.

One mornin' Huckabuck Marie and I sat outside on the family porch. She in the 'ole porch rockin' chair tippin' back and forth in the rhythm of an ocean tide slappin' against the floor boards and me tendin' to the plants.

"Sometime Mr. Washington need ta' say no to 'dem politicians and businessmen who's constantly sendin' him invitations," she said.

I listened, clippin' my plants that were over the window sill and the ones that were hangin' down from the top of the porch, almost reachin' the hand railin'. All the plants that were drapin' down from the top of the porch roof had formed a beautiful canopy. It was a porch of distinction, so much that the Outlaw house could be identified from a distance. This and Mama Tutu's good cookin' attracted the Sunday church crowd and provided cool shade for our many porch guests.

"You 'bout to drive me crazy screechin' across that board," complained Mama Tutu from just inside the doorway.

"If I didn't know that he was such a kindhearted man, I would think he was tryin' to be one of them politicians his self," added my mama.

"You sho' is smart not to say much most of the time, 'cause that is the most ridiculous thing I ever did hear," Mama Tutu said, referrin' to Mama's comment.

"He can't afford to say no now, with three new buildin's under construction," I chimed in.

"His schedule looks like a jigsaw puzzle," said Huckabuck Marie. "The months are split into weeks and the days are chopped up into hours. Some weeks, when he is in route to Chicago or Boston for one of those businessmen's conventions, he stops and visits three different cities on his way. The Boston trips he says are the most tirin'," she continued.

"I d'clare, must be somethin' we can do to hep' him," offered Mama Tutu.

"Why don't we give him an 'ole fashion Southern style Sunday afternoon picnic when he's back here in Granville?" asked Huckabuck Marie. "Accordin' to his book, he has two Sundays still free next month."

"That's goin' to take a lot of doin'," cautioned Mama.

"And who would be better fit to do it than us, Mama?" I asked with excitement.

"I know the man is a busy man, but one thin' fo' sho' he still likes to eat," Mama Tutu asserted. "Afta' travelin' all over up in de north, eatin' scones and drinkin' tea, he be longin' for some Southern style cookin'," she continued.

We all added our comments of agreement.

"Yeah, chile...Amen. Glooo...ry to God, purrrrfect!

"Furthermore, it'll be a good chance for him to officially introduce the missus," I said. "This may cut down the number of hussies he got to fight off every week!"

"I'll take the notes," said Huckabuck Marie. "Let's start with the guest list."

"That ain't hard," Mama Tutu replied, "all we have to do is send invitations to every colored family who owns land in Granville, then announce the picnic at church a couple of Sundays 'fo the picnic, and every other fool in town will be there." We all laughed.

We all agreed to keep the picnic as a surprise for Mr. Washington.

"Now all we need is someone to occupy him on the day of the picnic with some phony business from the school," said Mama.

"Oh yeah, that's the only way we can guarantee that he would be in town," I said.

I knew when they all looked at me, I was the one who would get that job and that I'd have the time of my life tryin' to outsmart him. I also knew that unless it involved the school it would, most likely, not work. It would have to be a serious problem in the school for him to cancel a scheduled engagement.

"I'll set up a sham appointment," said Huckabuck Marie, "and then we'll trick him into stayin' for a school emergency."

Creatin' the school emergency was my assignment.

Huckabuck's job was to provide a list of business associates of Mr. Washington. Mama Tutu and Mama agreed to arrange for the use of the church grounds and to provide the names of clergy who were his supporters. The ladies also agreed to help me design the caper, which would convince him to call off a meetin' and stay in Granville.

We wrestled half the night away tryin' to come up with a big enough emergency to make Mr. Washington stay a full weekend in Granville, in spite of the continuous flow of invitations from abroad. There wasn't much that could go wrong at the school because Mr. Washington was a meticulous organizer. He seldom left town without every detail already in place and a competent chain of command to handle any unexpected event. Whatever we did plan had to look like it occurred on the same day of the picnic and it had to demand his attention and require his presence.

With the help of Huckabuck Marie, we looked over his meetin' schedule. Mama Tutu knew that the best decoy would be somethin' that involved the fundin' for the Normal School. Then we came up with the idea that a telegram could arrive on the day before the picnic with a request from the General about the budget. Even though it was my job to prepare the budget papers we knew he would insist on reviewin' the copy. I would hold him overnight while I pretended to work on the draft. He typically combed through them like he was searchin' for fleas on a horse. He'd have to stay in Granville. I easily enlisted the support of my cousin Josh to rig up a telegram that he would then deliver. The mornin' befo' the picnic would be the best time to give it to Mr. Washington. The budget, we decided would look real official with the school trustee seal stamped at the top. It would advise him of a trustee meetin' for the approval of the budget. Of course, we would pretend that the meetin' was called together in response to the telegram to General Armstrong. Somehow we would have to get him to the picnic without him suspectin' anythin' about it. And it all had to run like clockwork on the same day of the picnic. We agreed on the strategy and set out on our charges.

I was a little scared. After all I had the most difficult task. I had to occupy him and then walk him through the fictitious telegram scam. He trusted me so much that the real problem was makin' myself lie to him. I know that he would be angry with me for interferin' with his schedule. Ordinarily, I'd rather eat poison berry pie than get between him and his travelin' plans. Lord knows I was the first to agree he needed a rest but just the thought of me lookin' him straight in the eye and fibbin'. I just couldn't see it.

Huckabuck Marie had lyin' down to a science so I leaned on her for lessons in the fine art of deceit. She promised to teach me the eye movements and ways to look coy and innocent at the same time.

"Don't worry." Her eyes narrowed as she said, "It's not as hard to do as you think."

It was an entire language that I had missed by growin' up in the church. Huckabuck Marie was like a chameleon; she could mask any emotion and amass an entire spectrum of sense and sensibilities. When she rubbed her tongue against perfectly lined teeth, she had a way of dismantlin' a crowd. This taught me that book knowledge and life skill are separate and sometimes not equal.

Durin' our plannin' meetin', Mama decided that it was better to keep quiet and just listen for orders, particularly from Mama Tutu. We all had one thing in common though and that was that we all loved Mr. Washington. So we exhaled a collective sigh and confirmed our resolve to surprise, delight, and honor him in the best way we knew how.

"Let's meet next week to review how the plan is progressin'," said Mama Tutu.

"Uh-huh," said Mama.

"Yes'm, said Huckabuck Marie and myself at the same time.

"Double dare and no tag back," I screamed, hittin' Huckabuck Marie on the shoulder.

"Ya'll settle down. We got work to do," Mama Tutu scolded with a cross glare of the eye.

We all laughed joyfully with lofty spirits so high with purpose that Mama Tutu's evil eye didn't even scare us.

Chapter XVI

Pansy's New Appointment

We were wonderin' why Mr. Washington called Mama Tutu to ask about the time she usually set dinner out.

"Do you normally serve dinner at two o'clock?" he asked.

Mama Tutu cocked an eyebrow as if to say don't challenge my schedule.

"Like clockwork," she answered.

"What about the second Sunday in August?" he added.

My birthday was comin' up so I thought he was tryin' to arrange our regular meetin' along with a special Outlaw dinner at the house. He ain't need to do anythin' special for me, 'cause workin' and studyin' under Mr. Washington was all the thanks I ever needed. He took a special interest in me, I knew that. He had watched me grow over the years from an energetic young pupil to what he called "a gifted scientist." Under his tutelage, I had earned his respect, and for me, he was God made man.

At the school the two of us worked side by side in the fields with a syncopated rhythm and unbridled speed. The other students had to rise up early and stay up late to keep up pace with us. I also helped recruit the newest member to the department who had just recently left the Shaw School of Botany to join the staff of the normal school. Mr. Washington maintained an organized system of checks and balances at the school by requestin' weekly updates from each department head. Because of his added travel demands, any time he was away he asked that I keep him informed of the progress on the farm in general and all the details discussed at these regular meetin's.

We all worked tirelessly and whenever he was gone, I made an effort to foster his spirit of cooperation. So while he was away I called the staff to one of those briefin's to report on the new recruit. I was so nervous my bladder suddenly gave alarm. After my announcement, I managed to slip out of the room to relieve myself. Once I left the room the staff burst into thunderous chatter and I could hear the excitement over the proposal I had made to invite the new scientific researcher to the school's agricultural department. Mr. Washington had already approved the invitation and was anxiously awaitin' the news of how the other staff members responded to the plans. I hadn't realized he had already returned from travel.

As I cut through his study, he was waitin' there. For me, each opportunity to meet with him, whether to discuss the school, troubleshoot problems, or design paths of expansion, was an opportunity to experience conscious contact with God as I understood him. He was sittin' in his study, a large, carpeted library room that connected his office and an experimental indoor plant laboratory I had designed. The laboratory which adjoined the lecture hall to Mr. Washington's office made it possible for me to short cut through his office without passin' the Board members in the hallway.

When I walked into the study he was sittin' in the big oak rockin' chair that was special made for him by one of the wood shop students. He had started to doze off. I tiptoed pass him and gingerly headed for the bathroom.

Quietly, I tried not to make a sound liftin' my petticoat, to hold it away from my body so it would not rustle and I could slip away without disturbin' him. His face was serene with a smile that you could not only see on his lips but also detect across his closed eyelids. The strong hands that were folded in his lap had opened many doors to me. I was so thankful to him for believin' in me. When I came back into the study I looked at him and thought, Now this is a man whose eager feet, which seem ready to stand at attention, will proudly, walk into the twentieth century. Gently I lowered myself into the seat in front of him, tryin' not to awake him. As he slumbered, and as I studied his face, hands, and feet, tears filled my eyes. I felt a tender devotion as I looked on silently adorin' while my mentor slept. I decided not to wake him and started to stand.

"Why end our meetin' before it starts," he said, openin' his eyes.

"Oh! Why sir, why—I… I…well, I thought…." I tried to explain with my stammerin' and fiercely uncoordinated tongue that I thought he was asleep.

"Actually I was sleepin' at first, my dear, but when I realized you were there, I simply let on that I was still asleep. I did so enjoy the silence with you."

I put my hand over my mouth as if that would hide my blushin' face.

"You needn't be embarrassed," he continued. "The silence is quite harmless and it is sometimes considerably more revealin' than chatter."

"Would you like to resume your nap then sir?" I asked hastily.

"No, certainly not. I believe we are scheduled for this time and I am most interested in your report, especially the news about the new chap," he replied. "Did the others take a likin' to his biography, or were they stubborn and ignoble as they usually are?"

"They were terribly receptive, sir. I think they were quite relieved I hadn't recruited another female agriculturalist." We both laughed.

"I've read his bio and he seems to be a fit addition to the staff, but what about him attracted him to you, Miss Pansy?"

"His practice in animal husbandry, sir. He is hopin' to increase our food supply of beef, mutton, and pork just by increasin' our breedin' animals."

"A botanist with animal experience. Might he hold some other attraction to you, Ms. Pansy?" asked Mr. Washington. "I dare say, it is not hard to imagine what attracted him to the Normal School?"

"You're quite correct sir, it was the farm school."

"I wasn't referrin' to the farm school, Miss Pansy."

"Oh surely, sir, with his background and research plans, it is certainly what convinced him."

"Are you quite sure?"

"Oh yes, sir."

"You wouldn't be keeping anything from me, would you, Miss Pansy?"

"Anythin' like what, sir?"

Mr. Washington got up from the rockin' chair and left it rockin' behind him as he walked toward me. He took my chin in the palm of his hand and lifted my face toward him and smiled.

"This is a very beautiful face," he said. "Any man as smart as this man sounds would look into this face and see the years ahead of long-lasting beauty in it."

I was beside myself by then. I wasn't normally shy, but I dropped my eyes and began to squirm a little in my seat. His compliment filled my very soul and I felt somethin' like a stream of liquid star dust pourin' through my body and flow all the way down to the tips of my toes.

"Your beauty," he continued, "is one of your many assets, but you must learn not to ignore its effect on the gentry."

I tried to compose myself with a weak smile, but I was really overwhelmed by his acknowledgement of my feminine virtues.

"I was born with a woman's body and a man's brain; that's my luck. You know, sir, I never saw fit to take up with woman's chatter, things of the kitchen, or raisin' chillun. Eva' time I take a likin' to a gentleman, I scares him away. Huckabuck Marie said I like to argue too much. Way I see, some men's talk is pure fiction. Just 'cause ya' got muscle in your voice don't make me believe no foolishness."

"It's okay, Miss Pansy, you can tell me. I'm sworn to secrecy."

In a gesture of placin' his hand on the bible that was on the table. He kept on smilin' and shook his head from side to side as he looked deeply into my eyes and sent another shock wave down to my toes. What he saw was not the

Pansy Outlaw who had forcefully maintained order among a staff of over twenty-five academically superior men. Not the woman who had enlisted and trained some of those men herself. Not the women on whose shoulders he was about to place the official responsibility of assistant school administrator. Instead he saw a troubled and confused child.

"What is it, Miss Pansy?" he repeated.

"Oh nothin' sir."

"Pansy!" he insisted, firmly and resolutely.

"It's not that important, sir. As a matter of fact, it shall not change anythin'," I responded.

"Well then, it will matter even less when you tell me."

He turned away from her and walked over to the mantle to take up his corn pipe and pack it with tobacco from the can sittin' next to it on the shelf. As he filled his pipe with tobacco he continued to speak with his back facin' me.

"Of course, you have to decide whether or not you wish for me to know."

There was a pregnant silence as Mr. Washington neatly arranged the tobacco in his pipe. He turned to search for the flint on the table next to where I was sittin'. I reached in my skirt pocket and pulled one out and gave it to him. He stood beside me as I stood beside him, lightin' his tobacco, and when it was fully ignited he held the pipe to his lips and then rested his other hand on my shoulder.

"I know when you are troubled, my dear."

He was always able to convey his sincerity and concern with the gentleness of his words.

"He has asked for my hand in marriage, sir."

Mr. Washington looked down at me with an amazin' gentleness, not skippin' a single beat and asked, "How then does that suit you, missus?"

"It does not, sir. I do not love him."

"I see," he replied. "And you think he is coming here primarily to do his wooing."

"Yes, sir."

"Uh...huh," he said slow and deliberate.

"What shall I do, sir? I know the school needs him very much. He is the most notable Negro botanist in the South. He has been invited to Shaw School of Botany in St. Louis and has selected to come here. Our staff have reached a unanimous agreement on this recommendation and we would be fools not to appoint him."

"Don't you worry, my dear. I did not intend for you to make any compromise of your personal integrity in order to obtain qualified staff for the school. I commend you on your clarity of heart and I will defend your honor to the utmost, you can be assured. But I like this chap all the more for his ability to discern a fine woman."

I sighed with relief, knowin' that I would be safe from feelin' obligated toward a man I didn't love for the sake of the school.

Mr. Washington sharply turned to the mantle to refill his pipe with tobacco. He looked back over his shoulder and said, "I like your spirit, Ms. Pansy. Putting the school first before your own personal satisfactions are the qualities that make an able administrator. You have just confirmed my instincts about the public announcement I am preparing."

I got a little uncomfortable. I knew it was no great noble sacrifice that made me deny Mr. Carver's proposal. It was much simpler than that. I had no love in my heart for the man.

"Announcement, sir?" I asked nervously.

"Yes, in a fortnight I shall be joining your family in the celebration of your birthday."

I was not surprised that Mr. Washington knew that I was havin' a birthday. In the sixteen years that we had known each other, he had never missed a single birthday celebration of mine. What could he be talkin' about? An announcement? What kind of announcement? I wondered.

"I shall take the opportunity to announce your appointment as the new agricultural department head. That is, of course, if you will accept."

I flopped back down in the seat and sat totally speechless. My capable and articulate mouth was ajar. My eyes were fixed on the head master as he spoke and not a sound could be produced.

"This would automatically place you second in command here at the Normal School."

Mr. Washington walked directly in front of me. He looked right down at me from what seemed like the top of a tall oak. He stood uncomfortably close and continued talkin' as he reached out for me.

"You, my dear, are the only person I trust so completely, especially for the occasions when I must travel. Which is far more often than I had expected, directly resulting from the appeals I have been making on behalf of the school. When I am away, I need to know that things at the school will continue on schedule. There is only one person who I am certain can give me that assurance. That person is you. In my absences..." he paused and then continued. "You do understand, don't you that, at times when I travel, you will need to assume the responsibilities of the headmaster?"

I took a very deep breath and stared blankly at his face. I know he was still talkin' but at that point I wasn't only dumb, I had gone tone-deaf. I couldn't hear anythin'. He pressed his strong and massive hand down on my petite sculptured shoulder, it was as though he were leanin' on me. I turned and looked down on it and breathed out a long and steady sigh. I am sure he could feel my hot and nervous breath on his hand.

"You can do it, Ms. Pansy. All you have to do is say yes. So what will it be?"

I paused while I tried to regain my composure, which I am certain he noticed had been completely lost. There was no measure, either, for the volcano of joy that was suddenly eruptin' inside of me. I searched in my mind for a way to express the feelin'. All I knew was that it was a feelin' much greater than love and instead of causin' further hesitation, I just said, "Yes."

I could think of little more to say. I put my hand on top of Mr. Washington's hand and repeated my reply, "Yes."

That night was rare and beautiful. Silver moonbeams brightened the room where I slept. I sat up starin' at the shadows of light draped across the settee. This must be what becomes of the silver linin', I thought.

Chapter XVII

The Birthday Party

Everyone was gathered around the table. The best silver had been placed meticulously in its proper position. The extravagant glazed ham that occupied the center of the table was flanked on both sides with delicately seasoned hens, all products of the agricultural school's farm. The intimate group of family and close friends sat with their heads bowed as Judd Outlaw blessed the food.

"In da name of the father, and of da son, and of da holy ghost," he started. "We come here today to celebrate the birthday of my baby, Pansy. We thanks you for all da food and 'specially for deez good people you done sent into our lives. I thank you for my family Lawd, and I's askin' you 'ta keep yo' eye on us 'cause we 'goanna keep our eye on you, 'cause we know we can't do nothin' without you. Bless this food and this house, Lawd, and all the peoples that is in it and that comes into it. We only ask fo' good health so we can do yo' work here on dis earth, Lawd. May we be yo' humble servants, Lawd, and continue to praise yo' holy name above all others and.."

"Amen," interrupted Mama Tutu.

By this time Josh was already pickin' green beans from the large servin' bowl next to his plate. Mama Tutu kept sayin' Amen very loud in attempts to end the blessin' so she could serve her feast. Huckabuck Marie appeared to be asleep and Mr. Washington was tryin' to motion to me so I could poke her before she fell forward into her plate. Mama was bowed in total reverence as though she was hearin' the voice of da Lawd himself instead of her husband.

Judd Outlaw continued, "Pour a special blessin' down on dis here gentleman, Mr. Washington, Lawd. He done a lot of good in dis town and we ask that you touch his life Lawd as we know you has already. Don't forget my family, Lawd, 'specially my dahlin' daughter, Pansy. She ain't perfect, Lawd, but she means well. Remember also my boy, Lawd, Little Luke, Lawd, tell him we still love him, Lawd."

Jasper Ale, who had come a little late and was standin' near the head of the table, behind Papa, was clearin' his throat, anxious to sit down since he had been standin' all day teachin' classes. This cue usually worked for Papa and today was no exception.

"We ask these blessin's in the holy name of Jesus," Papa said, endin' his long prayer.

A loud and thunderous "Amen" rang out from around the table and the clamor of silver and English china filled the dinin' hall. All of the vegetables were fresh from the garden. Most of them had come from Mama Tutu's garden but some of them were part of the late summer harvest of the normal school's agricultural program. Every dish was exquisitely prepared by Mama Tutu or under her intense scrutiny.

"These tomatoes taste like they were grown in southern Italy," commented Jasper Ale.

"I bet you won't find a woman in southern Italy who can stew 'em like this," scowled Papa.

Mama Tutu was so busy tellin' all the women what to serve first and how that she missed the compliment. Mama did catch it and corrected him promptly.

"Judd Outlaw! Those are my stewed tomatoes and, I declare, you should recognize them by now," she said.

"Oh, must be 'cause dey's fresh from Pansy's garden," he retorted.

"Judd Outlaw are you tryin' to avoid sayin' that you like somethin' I made," complained Mama.

"I agree," interrupted Mr. Washington, "they are mighty fine tasting, ma'am. Scrumptious I'd say, simply divine."

That was enough for Mama. She quieted down. The dinner ended with the joyful celebration of my birthday. A cake was placed at the center of the table with twenty-nine candles glowin' in the darkened room. Huckabuck Marie led the family in a round of "Happy birthday to you and may the good Lord bless you." The latter part was somethin' she made up spontaneously. Everyone cheered as I blew out all twenty-nine candles with one breath. When the lights were turned back on, I told everyone that it was Luke, who had helped me blow out all the candles, from the other end of the table. He had a look that showed he wasn't quite sure how he fit into the picture. After Papa had mentioned "Little Luke," I didn't want him to feel left out. Immediately, Mr. Washington tapped on a crystal glass with his spoon and the room was quickly hushed.

"I am honored to be among such friends and so I won't bore you with speeches. I wish to announce the appointment of Ms. Pansy Outlaw as the new head of the agricultural department at the Normal School."

The crowd responded with an inflated, "Ahhh!" Mr. Washington tapped the glass again to hold back any further outburst so he could continue his announcement.

"It is further noted that along with this appointment comes the role of assistant to the head master—" The dinner guest were ready to speak again. "And…" he tapped the crystal once more. "Whenever I am absent from the institution, she will become headmaster, eh…I mean, mistress, headmistress."

He nodded to Mama Tutu, who rushed over to him with an imported bottle of sparklin' wine. He held up the toast and she poured.

A brief silence followed his comments because the guests were waitin' to be sure he was finished. Then they all responded with raucous cheers and applause. Mama Tutu made her way all the way around pourin' into raised crystal glasses. Papa made the toast. "Here, here, ladies and gentlemen. I toast to the future success of the Normal School and the lifetime success of my beloved daughter, Pansy!"

"Hip hip hooray!" the cheers resounded.

I was delighted with the honor, with it bein' my birthday celebration and all. With somewhat of a whimsical and humble spirit, I graciously stood before my family and closest friends and cried.

"I do not want to do this. I feel so pitiful and this is such a happy time for me. You know I love you all but I couldn't have accomplished anythin' like this without you all. Mother, Father, thank you for the gift of life, and Mr. Washington, thank you for the faith you have in me."

Chapter XVIII

A Secret Liaison

Right after the party Huckabuck Marie and I retreated upstairs to my room so we could have our own private celebration. Durin' all the merrymakin' both of us had maintained poise and restraint. The minute the bedroom door closed behind us, we jumped up and down shoutin' joyously. We dance around in circles holdin' each other by the waist swingin' outward until we were dizzy then collapsed. The huge oval rag rug that covered the floor in front of my maple wood bed was hardly enough to soften the crash, yet we felt nothin' but utter delirium. As we regained our equilibrium we fell back against the bed frame and screamed some more. My room was far enough away from the dinin' area that our screams could not be heard. Huckabuck Marie reached down in the pocket of her dress and pulled out a flask containin' one hundred percent pure grain alcohol. She unscrewed the top and handed it to me.

"Here's to you kid," she smiled.

"What?"

"Just drink it," she said. "It'll calm you down."

She stared at me with a suspicious expression on her face, and after my brief hesitation, she said, "Go on, drink it. Bottoms up!"

I took two big gulps from the flask and turned to her with bulgin' eyeballs.

"Tell me, am I dreamin'?" I asked.

Huckabuck looked at me and responded, "If you are, I am too." She turned the flask up to her mouth and then held it out in front of both of us.

"Here, let's take a look." We put our arms around each other's shoulder and with our cheeks to cheeks touchin', Huckabuck pointed to the double image in the flask.

"Since you da scientist, you tell me. If we were dreamin', would we be seein' our reflection in this flask?"

"I think it is possible," I answered with an unbelievable clarity that, in seconds, would be lost for the night.

"Well then, take a few more of those gulps you're takin', and the whole damn flask will disappear."

"Now what do you mean by that?" I asked innocently.

Huckabuck took a swallow from the flask and said, "This stuff is guaranteed to make dreams come true."

We passed that flask back and forth for what seemed like an hour. Huckabuck Marie's glaze was now fixed on the rag rug. I had dropped the empty flask on the rug next to her body. She herself was lyin' across my torso. We were both fadin' fast into oblivion.

"How many pieces of rag do you think it took to make this rug?" she asked.

"A masked bug? Did you say you see a masked bug?"

"No, silly," she repeated with slurred speech. "How many rags to make this rug?"

"A hug, I'll give you a hug," I mumbled. I tried to reach my arms around Huckabuck Marie's neck and we both fell over on our side.

We burst out laughin' and continued laughin' incessantly at nothin' in particular.

The party ensued downstairs and we were not missed by anyone but Mama Tutu. After some time had passed, Mama Tutu decided to tip toe upstairs and see if she could locate the guest of honor. She carefully opened the door to my room and quietly stuck her head through the openin'. What she saw was me and Huckabuck Marie wrapped in each other's arms passed out and sprawled all over the huge rag rug cover on the floor at the foot of the bed. She gently closed the door and returned to the party in time to say goodnight to the last guest that was leavin'. From the porch she could see Jasper Ale walkin' down the dirt road.

"Good night, 'ole Jasper."

"Good night back to you, Mama T. Say goodnight to the birthday girl for me."

"I sho' 'nuff will, and don't you try to start somethin' you can't finish, you heah."

Jasper Ale waved his hand to let her know he heard her response. Mama Tutu watched until he disappeared in the night shadows. She closed the curtains and latched the door after him. From the looks of Huckabuck and Pansy, she figured that he would be the last guest leavin'.

"Ain't nobody else goin' nowhere tonight," she mumbled.

Chapter XIX

The Sunday Church Picnic
(In honor of Mr. Washington)

The field behind the church looked like a garden weddin' was about to take place. White cloth covered tables were scattered across the luscious lawn. An open pit was draped with beef, pork and chicken parts which sent an invitin' aroma through the air. Huge ripe watermelon slices were laid out in a floral design around a silver plated punch bowl that was filled with iced fresh lemonade. Mama Tutu and Mrs. Outlaw were busy in the church kitchen tendin' the pies and cakes, with Huckabuck Marie nearby, addin' salt seasonin' to the potato salad.

"Did someone ask you to do anythin' to that potato salad?" Mama Tutu scoffed.

"No, I just thought it needed a little more salt," answered Huckabuck Marie.

"She thought," mumbled Mama Tutu. "Somebody needs to get her out of here. She knows as much about cookin' as I know about drinkin'. With her numb taste buds, salt is probably the only thing she can taste."

"Oh Mama T, she's tryin' to help," said Mama.

"Yeah, help herse'f' to the potato salad!"

"You just don't like her, that's all."

"Well, I can't help that, cause even if me and her was the only two people in hell, I would still feel a chill around that gal," said Mama Tutu, under her breath. Then she went over to Huckabuck Marie and with a big smile she asked, "How does it taste?"

"It's just fine now," answered Huckabuck Marie.

"Just fine now," Mama Tutu mimicked.

"Why don't you take it all outside and set up the salad table with the fixin's and fresh pickles," Mama Tutu instructed.

Huckabuck smiled happily and arranged the potato salad, a bowl of freshly made mayonnaise, and a jar of pickled cucumbers on a large silver tray that she balanced above her head as she sashayed across the church yard. As soon as she left the kitchen Mama Tutu turned to Mama and said, "Don't let the screen door hit you where the good Lawd split you." Mama Tutu and Mama shared a howlin' laugh together for the first time in years.

In the meantime, Mr. Washington and I were waitin' at the Normal School for the board of trustees to show up for the, so-called, "emergency meetin'" we had telegraphed Mr. Washington about on Friday mornin'. Mr. Washington was nervously pacin' the floor in his study and I was waitin' in the library, watchin' and waitin' for the clock to hit high noon. Josh was waitin' also at the town post office for the clock to strike twelve, as planned, so he could send another telegraph to the school advisin' the two of a change in the meetin' place. The new meetin' place was the church where everyone would be waitin'. When the clock struck twelve, I walked by the school's postal room and at that moment the telegraph was comin' over the teletype. I stood there watchin' it as it typed out the message, which Josh and I had rehearsed: TO WASHINGTON ET AL BOARD OF TRUSTEE MEETING CHANGED TO FAITH UNITED CHURCH HALL TODAY AUGUST 14, 1895 SIGNED, REVEREND SMITH, CHAIRPERSON.

I carefully removed the message from the wiretap and took it directly to Mr. Washington.

"Sir, a wire just came in regardin' today's meetin'."

"Don't tell me it's been canceled after I changed my travel plans just for it."

"No, sir, it hasn't been canceled; it's been changed to a different location."

"Where in the dickens…. Let me see that please, Miss."

I handed him the paper with the bold face message written across two lines.

"How far is Faith United from here?"

"It's just over a mile run, sir. If you want, I'll saddle up a horse and buggy. We could be there in less than five minutes," I responded.

"Very well, but let's put a move on it. I do not intend to botch my perfect record of punctuality because of this foible."

"Yes, sir!" My excitement was ever mountin' as we were approachin' the climax of my caper. Things were workin' out accordin' to plan.

I ran out of the dean's buildin' and across the field to the stables, saddled Mr. Washington's black stallion, and hitched it to the two-seated buggy. When I arrived in the front of the buildin' again, Mr. Washington was waitin' out front. We rode to the church in record time. He looked over at me a couple of times durin' the ride and smiled in admiration as I cracked at the back of the stallion. We pulled onto the dirt road that circled in front of the church and then I pulled up to the garden.

"The fastest way to the hall is around to the side," I said.

Mr. Washington followed close behind me as we entered through the archway to the picnic grounds. A banner waved above the canopy that read, "Booker T. Washington Day, August 14, 1895." Children with bouquets full of flowers lined the garden path and as Mr. Washington and I walked pass them; they tossed petals at our feet. The band began a rousin' verse of "Hail, Hail, the Gang's All Here," and the full assembly of friends and well-wishers crowded around him and began to applaud. Mama Tutu pushed her way to the front of the folks gathered and grabbed Mr. Washington by the arm and scooped him away to the head table right in front of the bandstand. No sooner had he sat down, Reverend Smith arose with extended hands to quiet the ex-cited multitude and to give the blessin'.

A hush fell over the garden like a sunny day at dusk.

"With our heads bowed today, we give thee thanks Almighty God for all thy blessin's and for this opportunity to honor, in particular, his steward Booker T. Washington. We come today to express our appreciation to him for bringin' the wealth of education to this rural South. Our young folks stand in his pres-ence as a testimony of hope for the future of our race. He is a man who stands out in the dark night as a lone star of dignity and has brightened the way for us all. In the twenty years laboring and associating with him under all kinds of trials and conditions, I never heard him say or do an imprudent thing.[1] So with our heads bowed today we give thee thanks to God and ask his continued blessin's on our distinguished guest of honor, Mr. Booker T. Washington."

The reverend began to clap his hands and the crowd followed with hoots and cheers. Huckabuck Marie and I were over by the salad table beamin' with pride over the success of the whole affair. Mama Tutu and Mama were standin' in the kitchen doorway wavin' frantically tryin' to get our attention. When I finally turned and noticed them wavin', I heard them yellin', "Get the pies y'all come and set them out for dessert."

Poor Mr. Washington was still tryin' to figure out how he was goin' to fit the trustee meetin' in along with all this festivity. It wasn't until several minutes later that Josh explained everythin' to him, and only then did he realize that it was all contrived.

"Well, well, I guess I owe you one, Josh," he said after hearin' the scheme.

"No, not me, Mr. Washington. It was mostly Pansy's idea."

---

[1]The Booker T. Washington Papers, Vol.6 1901-2, Nov.6, 1901, letter from William Henry Baldwin, Jr. re: comments of Dr. Curry.

"For some reason I'm not at all surprised to hear that. I'll see to it that she is properly disciplined in the immediate future," he said smilin'. The band played a rousin' song of patriotic vigor. Mr. Washington bid me and Huckabuck Marie over to him, which we thought was so he could thank us. Instead, he ordered Josh to take Huckabuck Marie and he took me by the hand. Then he gestured to the band to really pump it up. Josh started out skippin' across the bandstand with Huckabuck Marie in tow. The next thing I know I was spinnin' around on my toes in the center of the hardwood stage. The crowd was cheerin' again and again while I was feelin' a little bit like a spinnin' top with no floor underneath.

"Okay, okay, that's enough," I yelled. "I cry uncle. Uncle! Uncle!"

The rest of the day we laughed and we played. Some of the children raced in potato sacks and four of the winners were crowned with wreaths made of sugar cane, which they promptly ate.

"Humph! In my life I forgot a lot of things but I never forgot August 14, 1895."

Chapter XX

The Normal School Family

Mr. Washington wanted to ensure that young members of his staff were fully supported so they would be able to concentrate wholly on developments at the school. Seein' how Josh took on his responsibilities with such tenaciousness, he felt that it was a good time, in fact an absolutely vital time for Josh to have a wife. He literally took this problem into his own hands and sent a letter to his own sister askin' her to send her daughter to Granville in the hopes that he could do a bit of matchmakin'.

"Dear Sister," he wrote, "I know you have struggled tremendously to provide a beautiful and stable home environment for my niece and nephews. I have tried to be a help to you where I could during your husband's fatal illness and consequential death. I have never asked anything in return and I don't ever intend to do so. What I am writing to recommend, and I hope you will agree, is that your daughter come South. This I feel will benefit all concerned. It will especially benefit my niece, your only daughter who is not yet betrothed. I would like her to visit here within the next fortnight."

The day after Mr. Washington sent the letter to his sister in Walden County, Virginia, he sent a message to the school post office for Josh to come to his quarters immediately followin' the last school bell of the day. Josh was usually too busy to notice the school bell, but that day he was waitin' for it to ring. When that bell rang he left promptly and half walked, half skipped nervously across the courtyard that joined the two buildin's. As he got closer to the buildin', he started walkin' slower and slower. His mind began to wonder and he heard a little voice inside his mind askin' questions.

What could this request for a meetin' mean? Have I done somethin' wrong? Millions of thoughts crossed his mind and he wondered out loud. "I hope I'm not in trouble?"

When he came up to the buildin' he stopped before enterin' it. He looked down at the ground in front of him and saw three acorns. He stooped down and picked them up and carefully studied them in his open palm. I wonder which one of these is goin' to be dinner and which one is goin' to be buried," he thought. Maybe all of them will be stored away for winter, his inner dialogue continued. Then again, one of them could become a tall oak tree.

He decided to take all of them in with him to meet with Mr. Washington, for good luck. He was hopin' that he was not goin' to have to face a reprimanded for some forgotten detail of his work. He hesitantly walked into the front door and down the long hall, slowly and thoughtfully circlin' the three acorns around in the palm of his hand. Faith, hope, and charity, he decided would be the meanin' of the acorns. He knocked on the door to the study. There was no answer. He clutched them in his sweaty palm and knocked again.

"Come on in, boy," said the fatherly voice of Mr. Washington. Josh was immediately relieved. This was not Mr. Washington's disciplinary tone. Nevertheless, he entered the room cautiously and quietly closed the door behind him.

"Good to see you, lad," Mr. Washington said cheerfully.

"Good seein' you too, sir," Josh timidly replied.

"Can I get you anything?" he asked.

He reached for the tobacco on the mantle of his study and offered it to Josh.

"How about having a smoke with me?"

"Much obliged, sir, but I wouldn't know how."

"Good. Good," Mr. Washington said. He walked over to Josh and gave him a robust pat on his back that knocked him forward two paces.

"That's my boy. What you lack in strength you make up for in virtue.

"Say, remember that letter I posted two days ago?" Mr. Washington asked.

"Yes sir, it went out on the mornin' coach yesterday just before I got the note to meet you today. Is somethin' wrong? I bagged and loaded it personally. Was there a problem? I'm sorry sir, I thought I…."

"Whoa, son, no need to get all riled up. Did I say something was wrong?"

"No."

Josh looked up at Mr. Washington with a puzzled look on his face.

"I mean, no, sir, you didn't."

"Right. Now, sit down and listen carefully," said Mr. Washington.

Josh selected the big cotton stuffed rawhide cushion next to the mantle and Mr. Washington sat in the rockin' chair. They both heard a knock on the door.

"Who is it?" shouted Mr. Washington.

"It's only me," said Huckabuck Marie pokin' her head in the doorway.

"Just sayin' good night and droppin' off the letter you dictated today for you to sign."

"Just put it on the table," he said, pointin' across the room.

Huckabuck Marie carried the letter across that room with her body and soul. The tight corset gave deliberate accent to her voluminous hips as she swayed from side to side past the hypnotic stare of the two men and over to the table. She placed it on the edge and it dropped to the floor. Both men jumped up raced across the room and banged their heads tryin' to pick it up. Huckabuck Marie bent down to pick it up and met her chest to their faces on the way back up. Huckabuck Marie did not flinch. The two men were left gapin' down the bosom of the most desirous women in Granville.

"Oh, I got it," she said coyly.

She handed the letter to Mr. Washington. Josh just knew somethin' was goin' on and what he could see was nothin' more than a smoke screen for what was really happenin'. He sensed it. There was no evidence of it yet, and he was as aware of it as he was of the acorns in his pocket. It's like they were hidin' somethin' and everyone knew but him. He felt awkward and out of place. He was somewhat unconnected from the situation yet at the center of its relevance. What made him anxious was the uncanny feelin' that he was being set up and for what he had no clue.

"If you could tell me straight away why you called me, sir, I'll be out of your way in a minute."

The unknowin' and the secrecy was drivin' him mad. Out of respect he could not ever show his anger to the headmaster, so he just shuffled and twitted a bit in one spot.

Mr. Washington shook his head at Huckabuck Marie as if to say, "Not now." Then Huckabuck Marie spoke. "I guess you won't need me now, so I'd like to be excused," she said.

Mr. Washington responded as if comin' out of a trance, "Yes, yes, of course, you may take leave for the night."

She lifted her petticoat high enough to expose her garter and walked so close to Josh she slightly brushed against his arm with her bountiful breasts. Then she sashayed back across the room. As soon as she left and the door closed behind her, the two men looked each other square in the eye deliberately holdin' in their laughter until they knew she had left the buildin'. Mr. Washington walked over to the study window and pushed the drape back just a little to make sure she was out of hearin' range, and then the two gentlemen howled like wolves.

"Now that's a woman," said Mr. Washington.

"I reckon I'd be scared to touch a woman like that," added Josh.

"Oh she ain't any different than any other woman," said Mr. Washington.

"Well there ain't no other woman I'd rather have," said Josh.

"Then surely you can have her," Mr. Washington said.

"What do you mean, I can have her?"

"Well, what I mean is that I can get you a woman who is going to turn out just like that."

Mr. Washington pointed out of the window toward Huckabuck Marie. "But you get to have her before she gets like that and that way you won't be afraid to touch her by the time she gets like that."

Josh nods his head greedily, smilin' in agreement but still not sure what he was agreein' to. Mr. Washington motioned for him to sit down on the settee.

"You know the letter I sent to my sister today?"

"Oh yes, sir."

"I've asked her to send my niece for you to consider for a wife."

"A wife!" exclaimed Josh. "Why, the last time I saw her she was eight years old!"

"I know, son, and that would make her perfect for marriage now," replied Mrs. Washington.

"That's why they call it sweet sixteen, isn't it?"

"I don't know if I'm ready to start no family, sir," Josh answered.

"We're already family here at the Normal School. You won't be in it alone. It'll be like an addition to the family."

Josh stood straight up and was pacin' back and forth across the room as he listened. He juggled the three acorns in his pocket clockwise around the palm of his hand usin' the thumb and the forefinger to rotate them.

"You're doing a fine job here. Your future is secure. I can tell by the way you was eyeing Mame Huckabuck, if you don't get a wife soon, there's going to be trouble for you down South."

They laughed together again. Mr. Washington pointed toward the belted section of Josh's trousers.

"You can let that drive you crazy, or you can use it for the purpose it was given to you."

Josh sat down again and took the three acorns out of his pocket. He stared at them in the palm of his hand. Maybe this was a sign, he thought.

"Do you really think I'm…I mean, what kind of father is a postal clerk?"

"You mean a postal director," corrected Mr. Washington.

"Director?" Josh squealed.

"That's right, son. That'll be your new post right after the wedding."

"Weddin'? Suppose I don't like her?"

"You don't have to like her. You have to love her, and the rest will come with the new baby."

"Baby? Holy cow!" said Josh whirlin' around on his heels. "I don't know a thing about babies."

Civilized Blacks • 115

"It's really going to be all right Josh. Besides, Mama Tutu will help you through the first dozen."

"What?"

"Just joking," laughed Washington. "Just joking."

"You have a few days to think about all this. My niece will be coming in a fortnight, and I hope your decision is a wise one."

"Hold it, are you tellin' me that in a two weeks I could very well be an old married man?"

"I'd rather think of it this way. In two weeks, without any of the characters changing in this room, I could be standing next to the post office director who has just taken on a new wife," Mr. Washington said.

"Holy Jesus!"

Mr. Washington took Josh's thin shoulders in his hands.

"Look son, you have a good future here and you are not built for the fields. You're a man now and you need a woman. It's as simple as that."

He continued with one arm around the shoulder of his frail student trainee while walkin' him steadily toward the door.

"Nothing in life comes for free, you know. This is the kind of opportunity that will probably never come again. I can only open the door for you, son, but you have to walk through it alone."

Josh stood in front of the door opened by Mr. Washington and felt an overwhelmin' weakness in his knees. He struggled to force his mind to review all that had been revealed to him in the past hour. Within seconds he realized that he was blind with anxiety. With his chin sunk deep into his chest, he walked through that door and slowly slipped his hand into his pants pocket feelin' around for the acorns.

"I'm about as close to feelin' like a husband as these acorns are to bein' oak trees," he said to himself.

Chapter XXI

A Bedtime Lullaby

It was a bad marriage from the start. Josh's new wife had borne him a child within the first year. Mr. Washington kept his promise and Josh became postal director at the Normal School. He did more than he promised and made Josh's wife a teacher in the homemakin' class. Mr. Washington made arrangements for Mama Tutu to live in with Josh and his new wife durin' the week. She returned to the mansion only on weekends. The newborn was her weekly charge, and for her it was the pinnacle of joy. On the contrary, for Josh's wife it was a constant reminder of her incompetence as a mother.

"Why does the baby coo and gurgle so when that 'ole woman is around?" she asked.

No one really knew how much she felt inferior as a mother. Only Josh knew, and every little complaint that she could think of about Mama Tutu, she would make whenever she and Josh were alone.

"She fusses with that chile a little bit too much for my likin'. Don't she ever put her down?"

"We should be thankful they get on so well, don't you think?" asked Josh.

"Obviously what I think don't matter much around here," was her angry reply.

By then the Outlaw house had extended into the Normal School. Both Josh and I had permanent residence there. With my new responsibilities and the frequency of Mr. Washington's travels, it made it necessary for me to move into the dormitory. Because of my position I was assigned to the prestigious accommodations at the vestry, which, though part of the dormitory, was a separate buildin' that sat beside the girl's wing of the residence hall.

Josh's house was one of the early buildin's that had been erected by students as part of a construction project curriculum and was recently used as a clubhouse for the small military guard at the school. The air force guard had grown so large that a new and bigger buildin' had been built to replace the old one for the twelve-member squadron that had grown into a small regiment. The stately new military headquarters was built to state-of-the-art specifications, which included its own commercial size kitchen and mess hall.

These changes were tantamount to the growth and expansion of the normal school. Josh had married Mr. Washington's niece and they had started a family. Mama Tutu regularly came often to care for their new daughter. It was particularly her regular presence at the Normal School that made it seem like an extension of the Outlaw household. For everyone except the one person she was there to help, this presence was a welcomed addition to the school community.

"You's a pretty little thing," Mama Tutu said as she bundled baby Josette in her winter blankets and laid her down to rest. She went about the nursery arrangin' the fall flowers, dustin' the cabinets and hummin'. Every few minutes she walked over to the cradle and gave it a nudge to continue the rhythm of the gentle rockin'. The bright room was full of sunshine and the smells of winter. Crisp white curtains hung from the tall imperial windows of the estate. The aroma of soup from the kettle hangin' over the fireplace downstairs filled the rooms. Inside the nursery the whisperin' scent of lilac and fresh cotton. Pink satin crochet lace-lined pillows were tossed around the cradle. The air was filled with the fresh green cooin' sounds of new life. Mama Tutu leaned over the cradle.

"Who you talkin' to, little lamby poo? Is you seein' spirits? If you is, tell 'em hi fo' me."

Baby Josette kicked excitedly at the sound of Mama Tutu's voice. Her tiny feet beat furiously against the pink fluffy baby blanket.

"You sho' got a lot a spunk for somebody only been here six months."

She turned Josette over on her stomach and began pattin' her on the back with gentle and rhythmic strokes. She sang her my favorite lullaby.

"Oh my baby, my little baby. Oh my dahlin' sweet little girl. Sweet little, sweet little, sweet little girl. Strong and smarter than any in the world."

After only a few verses, Josette fell into an angelic sleep.

While the baby slept Mama Tutu had just enough time to mix dough for the dinner rolls. It was unusual for weekday supper to include rolls, but tonight was special. Mr. Washington had just returned from a travelin' business convention and tonight was his first visit to his grandniece. Dr. Carver had killed a hen from the chicken coup and it was bastin' in seasonin's all day. Any part that was not on the roastin' post was in the soup. As soon as the sun dropped a little in the sky, Mama Tutu strapped the baby around her waist and went out to the garden to pick fresh greens. It was a life that she loved. She was happy with the abundance that nature provided and with the surroundin's of beautiful buildin's in elegant and classic style.

Josh's wife apologized to Mama Tutu constantly for everythin' she had to do. Secretly she wanted to be the one doin' it all. She saw Mama Tutu bent over in the kitchen garden at the side of the house when she was walkin' home from school. She dropped her sewin' basket and ran to help.

"Here, here Mama Tutu," exclaimed Josh's wife, "you shouldn't be bendin' over. It's not good for you. I'm terribly sorry that you didn't wait for me to do this for you I just don't understand.

Oh dear, you'll catch your death out in the cool fall air," she complained.

"I'm fine, chile, you just go on in. You must be achin' all over after standin' over them machines all day. 'Sides, I's 'da only one knows the greens I want and the ones I don't."

That night after dinner Mama Tutu insisted on cleanin' up everythin'.

Josh showed Mr. Washington pictures of himself when he was the eighth grade wrestlin' champion.

"You were quite threatening as a teen, I see," commented Mr. Washington.

"Yeah," answered Josh sullenly.

"By the looks of you now, I would have never guessed you were that big."

Josh shrugged his shoulders. Mr. Washington put the brass-framed picture of Josh back on the magnificently ornate mahogany cabinet standin' within arm's reach of the table.

"Let's see what ya got," Mr. Washington said, puttin' his elbow down on the table and his open palm pointed in Josh's direction.

"Nawh, it's okay"

"Come on, you have a thirty-five year advantage."

Josh leaned forward, placed his elbow besides the one waitin' and clasped his opponent's hand.

"Ready, set, go."

Neither arm moved as the two men applied more and more pressure.

We were all gathered around and I was havin' fun with the baby. I held her playfully above my head swayin' back and forth while I hummed children's melodies. Huckabuck Marie, who would rather be tarred and feathered than miss an Outlaw family dinner, impatiently waited for her turn with the infant.

"Hey, you've had her far too long," said Huckabuck, "and if you don't quit shakin' her like that, she's goanna throw her dinner up all over you. And it'll serve you right for hoggin' her like that."

"Pipe down, Huck, she's nothin' to you, remember. You've got no rights."

"I beg your pardon, have you forgotten that I am the godmother?"

"That still doesn't give you rank over a blood relative and sense when you believe in God."

"My beliefs ain't got nothin' to do with it, give her to me!"

"No, you just wait."

"Now, now, you two," interrupted Mama Tutu, "that's a newborn baby you're tusslin' over, not a field chicken."

"Okay, here, you can hold her but be careful," I warned.

"Look who's talkin'," replied Huckabuck Marie, takin' the child into her arms.

"Let me rescue you from 'dat wild women, you precious little dumplin'."

The baby nestled snugly against her godmother's bosom.

"See she already feels better."

"Well look a here," said Mama Tutu. "You the last person I would expect to have that effect on a baby."

"Babies know," said Huckabuck. "Babies know," she repeated.

Mr. Washington was gainin' the advantage over Josh. Josh's hand was pushed halfway back. He tried desperately to make a comeback. His arm shook from the strain of forcin' against Mr. Washington's weight. Finally his whole hand dropped backward and hit the table. Josh let out an exasperated sigh.

"Best out of three." said Mr. Washington right away, replacin' his elbow on the table.

"No, that's okay. You won."

"Oh, come on; let's see you work up a sweat this time."

"No, really. I'm a bit tired tonight," Josh said.

"Everybody's tired tonight," Mama Tutu said as she walked past Josh.

She was busy cleanin' up the leftover vittles. The icebox was so full of meats from the farm school there was hardly room for anythin' else. Mama Tutu yelled from the pantry,

"Y'all can tell Dr. Carver to stop killin' animals for me, 'cause I can't fit no more in here."

She came into the dinin' hall mumblin'.

"'Sides I done everythin' I can, and in spite of all 'deese chickens he keep killin', Miss Pansy ain't no closer to marryin' him than heaven is to hell."

She came back in laughin' to gather the last of the dirty china from the table and take them out to the washtub. She heard Huckabuck Marie and I were back to fightin' over the baby in the family room.

"You've had her long enough," I said.

"Now you just bring me back my baby, Miss Huckabuck," Mama Tutu firmly said.

Carefully handlin' little Josette over to Mama Tutu, Huckabuck Marie went into the dinin' room to say goodnight to Josh and his wife. I followed behind her.

"Good night, ya'll. Thanks for the wonderful little bundle of joy," said Huckabuck Marie politely.

"Mama T, you did it again on the food," I added.

I stretched my arms around my beloved Mama Tutu.

Both of us left reluctantly after a long ritual of embraces. Mr. Washington followed close behind us.

Mama Tutu stood in the doorway wavin' goodbye. Mr. Washington walked proudly down the front steps with one lady on each arm.

"Wave bye, bye to yo' uncle, chile," said Mama Tutu, holdin' the infant's hand out from the quilted bundle.

Josh and his wife never knew what to say when they were alone together. Josh dipped his index finger in the half full glass of water and circled the rim, makin' whimsical sounds on the top edge of the crystal.

Mama Tutu returned to the solemn atmosphere of Josh and his wife.

"I got more energy than a runaway slave," she announced.

"Why don't you two love birds get to workin' on my great-grand niece's little brother! All the guests are gone and I sho' don't need no entertainin'."

"But I insist on helpin'," said Josh's wife.

"Help with what? All I have to do is put out the fire. You concentrate on puttin' out ya'lls. I'll bring the baby up after I rock her to sleep."

Josh had set six glasses side by side and was creatin' a melody with various quantities of water in each. His young wife started toward the spiral staircase and looked back at him.

"Josh Ambush, you quit playin' with them crystals and come on up to bed this instant."

Josh didn't stop right away.

"Do you hear me!" she shouted.

"Okay, I'm comin'." Josh went first to Mama Tutu and the baby.

"Give daddy a kiss," he said to the infant.

He kissed Mama Tutu on her cheek. "Goodnight, grandma," he said and turned to follow his wife upstairs.

Mama Tutu sat down in front of the open hearth with baby Josette, wrapped in swaddlin' covers and laid the baby face-down across her lap. As she rocked back and forth, she patted gently and tenderly on the baby's back. The soothin' rhythm gave birth to a song.

"Oh my baby, my little baby. Oh my dahlin' sweet little girl. Sweet little, sweet little, sweet little girl. Strong and smarter than any in the world."

Mama Tutu could rock the devil to sleep with that song she sang. Gradually the song faded. She began to hum. Then instead of pattin' the baby, she just rocked and tapped her foot. All of the movement ultimately dissolved into warm glowin' stillness by the open fire.

When it is nightfall at the normal school it is so quiet, you can hear a pin drop. So when Josh heard the loud bangin' on his door, he jumped up immediately and ran to the bedroom door. He opened it and a huge flame burst into his face. He slammed the door shut, and startled his sleepin' wife. As she woke up to the sounds of crashin' glass, they both heard a loud voice screamin'.

"Anybody in there?"

"Get up," yelled Josh. "There's a fire."

Josh's wife leaped out of bed and ran toward the door. Josh blocked her. "No," he said.

She attempted to get bye him but he held her back.

"No, I said."

"My baby!" she yelled in a panic. They heard voices from outside beckonin' them to get out. Together they ran over to the window and shouted.

"Help! Help!" Their screams could be heard echoin' through the night.

"Get out. Jump!" in unison the crowd screamed.

I heard all the commotion from the other side of the field and hopped into my old farm trousers, grabbed the shawl hangin' by the door, and ran like the dickens toward the burnin' house. I saw a big orange ball of fire from the other side of the field. As I got closer, I could see flames snappin' against the windows; I didn't have time to think. Immediately I bolted toward the door. The handle was so hot I had to use the end of my shawl to hold the latch. Once I got in I covered my face with it to filter out the chokin' billows of smoke risin' up from the burnin' wood floors.' I strained to see through my shawl with stingin' eyes. I yelled out for Mama Tutu and got no answer. I raced through the entrance hall toward the parlor. My foot hit a bundle on the floor and I tripped. It was the body of the baby, wrapped and smolderin' on the floor by the doorway to the sittin' room. She had been sheathed inside her blanket. I threw the blanket off of her and covered her with my shawl. It was impossible to breathe so I had to leave without findin' Mama Tutu. I'll never know how I kept from catchin' on fire myself.

When I got outside the fire team had arrived and I put the baby down on the grass. They took her. Although I couldn't stop coughin', I tried to return to find Mama Tutu and two firemen grabbed me by my arms, one on one side and one on the other. I struggled to free myself but I couldn't. They tried desperately to pull me away from the house and I wouldn't let them. Cries were piercin' the hollow night skies. A second team of firemen ran to stand below the window as a crowd gathered on the front lawn. Extended hands waved from the crowd in the amber light, the dancin' flames flickered in the faces starin' up.'

"Jump, jump!" they all screamed again in unison.

Smoke began to fill the top of the house. The room was gettin' dark with smoke. I could hear the couple fightin' for air through their coughs. Josh ripped off a piece of his wife's gown and put it over her mouth. You could see from below that her eyes were furious with fear. Josh pulled open the window and looked down to a huge military tarpaulin held in place by several of the military students.

"First the misses," he heard a voice yell.

The fire squadron entered the house, but the flames were too thick and they had to come back out.

The young couple just stood in the window. Black smoke was fillin' up the room. The brigade captain yelled up to the window.

"There's no other way out, Josh! You have to jump!"

They grasped for one another holdin' on to the upper ledge of the window. The crowd below kept wavin' them down and callin' out to them, "Jump! Jump! Jump! Jump!"

Josh told his wife to go first. She clung to him desperately with her frail hands graspin' at his neck and wouldn't let go.

"We'll jump together!" Josh yelled down.

"Hurry, get some more men around the blanket," the fire chief yelled.

"You're crazy, it won't work," the captain yelled back.

"Where's our baby?"

"The baby's out!" I looked up in terror.

"They're goin' back in with fire suits, but the smoke may overtake you by then," yelled the fire chief.

"Then it'll have to work, we don't have a choice," Josh said.

Seein' the look of panic in his wife's eyes and the feelin' of her tremblin', wet, clammy hand stayed etched in his memory forever. She wouldn't jump, so they leaped from the window together.

"Ready, set, go," he whispered in her ear.

Those were his last words to her.

The next thing I knew I was lying in a bed at the infirmary.

"We had to knock you out," said the fireman who was left to guard me.

"Where am I?"

"You're in the infirmary."

"Where's the baby?"

"I'm sorry, mame. The baby didn't make it."

"But I got her out! Where is she?" I asked, tryin' to get up.

"I'm sorry, mame, but you have to rest now."

"Where is the baby? Where's the baby? I got her out! Where is she? Is that so hard to answer?" I screamed.

"Mame, the baby was already gone when you brought her out."

"Oh, God, I had her. I had the baby in my arms! What are you sayin'? Are you sayin' she dead? She dead?"

He nodded yes.

"And Mama Tutu—what about Mama Tutu?"

"She's in the next room."

"Take me to her," I said getting' up from the bed.

"Doctor said you have to rest, mame," he answered holdin' me down.

"I gotta see Mama Tutu." I leaned forward and pushed him away.

"Can't let you do that mame," he said, tightenin' his grip, "besides she's not..."

"Don't say it," I screamed and fought back the tears. "Please...don't tell me that she's...."

"No, mame, it's not that. She isn't conscious, and it doesn't look good."

"Oh no," I said. "God, no."

I let go and started sobbin'.

Chapter XXII

The Mourning

NEWS HEADLINE:
CHILD DIES, GRANNY LIVES; WIFE PLUNGES TO HER DEATH.

Four persons battle flames and only two survive," read the first line of the Granville Press.

It was assumed that Jasper Ale who, along with bein' the town historian and the church deacon, would be in charge of arrangin' the burials. Everybody around town was talkin' about the burial. The big question was whether the infant and the mother would be buried in the same casket. The family decided to put them in separate caskets and bury them together in the ground.

"Who makes all those dreadful decisions?" asked Huckabuck Marie, bitin' into one of the apples from a donated fruit basket sittin' at Mama Tutu's bedside.

"Shh," I quipped. "Good Lawd! Don't you know sometime people in a coma can still hear and you 'bout to bring her out of de coma, crunchin' on that apple like that. "Please close your mouth, will ya? If she could talk," I said, noddin' toward Mama Tutu, "she'd tell you how much like a pig you sound chewin' with your mouth open. Look, she's tryin' to open her eyes."

"How can you see her eyes under all those bandages?" Huckabuck Marie asked.

"Huckabuck Marie, will you hush up?"

"Can't you jus' say you don't know?" Huckabuck Marie asked, still chewin' with her mouth full of apple.

"Besides, for your information, not that it matters to you, the whole Virginia segment of the family will be arrivin' on the evenin' coach, and 'dem apples you eatin' is for Mama Tutu's guests."

"When did you hear that?"

"Jasper Ale received the wire this mornin'."

I spoke without takin' my eye off of Mama Tutu, not even blinkin'.

"Shame Mama Tutu was so tired she fell asleep watchin' that evil women's baby. That whole day she was cookin' and cleanin'. She never put little Josette down a minute, lessin' she was sleepin'. She even carried her out in the fields.""You know how Mama Tutu gets when Mr. Washington comes back from one of those trips up North," I said. "She acts like she's a human threshin' machine."

"Right until she sits down at the end of the day. I've seen her noddin' a plenty at dusk sittin' in the rocker on the porch."

"That must be what happened," I said. "The fire chief said a spark must'a flew out of the hearth and caught on her skirt. Mama Tutu was overcome by smoke before she knew anythin' and dropped the baby. Her little swaddled body rolled away from the flames, which is how I managed to get to her."

"I know you must be terrified, but she'll pull through," Huckabuck Marie said, reachin' over to hold my hand.

"I can't believe this is happenin'," I said. "Can you?"

"No."

I looked out at Jasper Ale, who was standin' in the hall outside the sick room.

"If it were not for him, you, and Mr. Washington, I wouldn't know what to do," I cried out.

Mr. Washington walked in the room at the moment I mentioned his name.

"How is she?" he asked.

We watched helplessly over Mama Tutu as he walked up to the other side of the bed. He bent down to kiss her wrapped forehead.

"Has she spoken, yet?" he asked.

"No, not a word," replied Huckabuck Marie.

"She did try to open her eyes," I quickly added.

"She's definitely not out of the woods yet," he said. "She's probably still in shock. I'll order a twenty-four hour watch. You women go and get some rest."

Still, three days later, no change. I walked into her room hopin' for a sign of life. Mama Tutu lay lifeless on her sick bed and I noticed that the nurse solemnly shook her head upon leavin' the room to refill the water jug.

"It doesn't look good," she said softly as she left.

I slumped over the foot of the bed and wept. All hope was fadin'. The fruit basket was nearly empty. Many of the town's people had come to pay their last respects to Mama Tutu. In another two days they would bury Josh's wife and child. There was a dark cloud over the whole town. Every single man, woman, and child was mournin' this tragedy. In times like this it was Mama Tutu who could always corral the community. Now she, too, was a victim of disaster. Mr. Washington had left and returned with a report from the doctor.

"I don't want you to be alarmed," he said.

"What?"

"I just spoke to Dr. Carver who visited here this afternoon. She hasn't shown any decline. She is holdin' steady. We just have to wait."

"Is there somethin' he can give her to bring her back from this dreadful silence?" I asked.

"I'm afraid not, but maybe it will comfort you to know," replied Mr. Washington, "that silence isn't usually dreadful."

"It may not be for her, but it is for me. Oh! Mr. Washington I can't bear the thought of her leavin' me."

"She loves you so much, Miss Pansy, she would never willingly leave you. If she does, it will only be by God's will and not by hers. Now, do you trust me?"

"You know I do, Mr. Washington, more than anyone I know."

"Then trust what I am saying to you now. God's will is intended only for good. Sometimes the good is impossible for us to see. One thing for sure, we all have to go some day. You don't have to worry, we can keep her here at the infirmary for as long as you like."

"Thank you, this is where she would want to be, sir," I responded.

"I feel so deserted. I don't know who I am without her," I moaned.

"I still wonder, Mr. Washington, if she ever questioned her identity, her values, and her place in life?

"Perhaps at some time," he answered, "but not anymore. You can see that in the serenity of her face. Try not to worry, whatever happens, when her time does come, whatever you need, I'll see to it that you get it. You trust me don't you?"

"Yes, sir. I do."

"I know you don't want to hear this, but remember the mule drawn carriage that she always said she wanted to carry her up to Zion?"

"Yes, sir. I do."

"Dr. Carver is making arrangements so that she will have it for her journey."

"Yes, sir. Oh, thank you, sir."

The room was deathly quiet after that. Lost in thought and preparin' for the worse. I sat by her bedside starin' at the pine wood floor. Mr. Washington looked around the room, makin' sure everythin' was clean and ordered. He ran his finger along the windowsill checking for dust. The sun drenched flowers stood majestically in the delicately painted Chinese vase sittin' on the top of the nurse utility cart. The stillness and radiance of the moment was suddenly interrupted by the scratchy sound of a rusty and raspy voice vibratin' through the whole room.

"T'aint dead yet."

I jumped out of the chair so fast that I knocked over the vase which went crashin' to the floor.

"Oh God, she's alive, she's alive!" I exclaimed.

I couldn't believe it. I had never prayed so hard for somethin' before or since, and my prayers had been answered. We stood there amazed. She coughed a little and then slapped her hands together.

"You just gonna stand there? Snap out of it and get me some water," she said through her coughs.

"Mama Tutu! She's back," I cried out to Mr. Washington.

He drew the curtain to let more of the light enter the room and whispered loud enough for her to hear.

"You sure can't stop a legend 'til it's done doing what it has to do, even if it does get a little cooked in the process," Mr. Washington remarked.

In the weeks followin', Mama Tutu got stronger. The infirmary received a governor's citation for their successful treatment of her burns. After nine weeks of rehabilitation, Dr. Carver agreed to allow Mama Tutu to have week-end visits home. It was such a long wait, yet she finally did come home to stay. I was glad she did, 'cause what happened next was more than I could have handled alone.

Chapter XXIII

Sunset

The thought of losin' Mama Tutu was too much to bear. I was still exhausted from the long journey back from death's door. So when the news of Mr. Washington's illness started buzzin' through the halls of the normal school, I had to pull the strength from inner resources I didn't even know I had deep down inside. Urgent reports arrived by the "phony express," which is what we called the word of mouth rumors that always beat the real pony from up North. The Boston Public newspaper had a front-page story, and I knew it must be serious when I saw that an official correspondence arrived at the Normal School post office describin' it.

Mr. Jasper Ale came hobblin' over to the Normal School to hear the latest from what was sent in the mail. I saw him comin' through the tall aristocratic window of my dormitory suite. Customarily, I went out to meet guests who came to my quarters, but today I stood at the window and watched sternly as he approached. I found it strange he would come to me. He was the one who was least supportive of my appointment as dean. I stood there rememberin' the day I jolted out of his classroom like a scalded cat. Recallin' all the discouragin' things he had always said. How he had mimicked my aspirations and scorned my attendance at the Normal School. Now he was comin' to me for information. I watched his frail body struggle with each step. I wondered if he would even make it to the front door. His weary bones looked ready to fall into a pile while he feebly grasped for each breath. His weakness gave me strength. I had survived his reproachful forecasts. As he stood tappin' faintly on the door, I had a mind to leave him out there, half chokin' from a lack of air. Justice would have been served, I thought, but he didn't fall. He kept on bangin' on the door like a prodigal son returnin' home. I reluctantly opened the door. He looked ready to collapse in the doorway from the heat.

"Howdy do, ma'am," he said, liftin' his hat all in one harmonious gesture of sound and motion.

"I come for 'de news. I figured they done told you, 'cause you 'bout the second most impoten' person in this here school besides Mr. Washington."

"Oh really, and what makes them think that?"

"Since eva' time I ask a question folks say you de one with the answer about Mr. Washington's news. I come here today for de answer," he said.

I stood in the doorway staring blankly at him.

"Didn't Mama Tutu teach you any manners, Ms. Pansy?"

"Manners, I thought, is not coming to someone's home uninvited."

"Ah, the great historian searchin' for answers," I mumbled, peeping through the stained glass window that bordered the door. He removed his hat and grabbed his throat in an act of sheer desperation.

"I'm mighty thirsty, Ms. Pansy," he said.

"I'm indisposed." I spoke through the door.

"What would make you leave thirty students midday to come all the way over here?"

"I come to find out de news about Mr. Washington," he said.

He stood bent over at the top of the stairs leaning against the door frame; a pitiful site.

"How is it you come here unannounced?" I asked.

"Excuse me, missus, but I know you be the one who would get the information first from up the road," he answered.

"I would think if Mr. Washington wanted you to know something, he would contact you directly. Don't you?" I continued with my questions.

"Ms. Pansy, I really don't see why you can't just open 'dis door."

"Let me think. First you break my afternoon nap, then you try to force your way into my home while I am scantily dressed, and then you insult me and Mama Tutu, and you wonder why you ain't gettin' a warm welcome. Swallow some of that pride while I get my cloak. It may quench your thirst in the meantime!"

"Now look here, young lady. I held my peace all these years and you about to force me to break my silence. Can't you give me a simple answer ever!" he screamed as I turned away from the door and announced, "Door's open."

"How would you like a cold glass of lemonade," I replied coolly, as if he had never asked a question, which he hadn't.

He really wanted to jump right to the facts, but he was terribly thirsty after the walk up the road. I turned away from him and walked toward the cooler. I inquired about his health very quietly as I walked away. I could see his reflection in the silver plated mirror hangin' on the wall. He was strainin' to hear.

"What was that, ma'am?"

I said, "You don't look well, Mr. Jasper. Have you been ill?"

He shuffled his feet back and forth like he was tryin' to steady himself. Soon as he got his footin' he leaned against the doorframe.

"I've been better. I guess a man ain't made to last forever. If you don't mind, ma'am, I'll take a seat right here on the windowsill. I don't mean to take up much of yo' time."

"It's fine, Mr. Jasper, I've been waitin' for the day that you would take any time with me at all. I don't mind; in fact, I am rather flattered."

I gave him the lemonade, bowin' as I did. I examined him carefully, takin' in the whole of his worn out sullen face three-quarters covered in a sprinkle of salt and pepper whiskers. His dusty old smell confirmed that he had seen his better days. Just a bag of bones, I thought, and I'm so glad I lived to see it. He took long and noisy gulps of the drink, and then sighed. As he leaned back against the window box, his head tilted up with his hands resting on the top of his cane. He ventured to make another stab at getting' the news update.

"Well, I'm here to get de news. When will Mr. Washington be comin' back to town?"

"I'll be right there, Mr. Jasper. I think I'll pour one for myself," I said.

I walked away casually. From the pantry, I took a good hard look at him through the drawin' room curtain. He sat limply on the windowsill, his forearm restin' on his cane. I reflected on certain people like Mr. Jasper who could have destroyed my dream if it were not for the one giant of a man who providence had led to me.

Returning to the room, I unleashed my fury. "You really have your nerve even coming here." I entered the room partin' the curtain, exposin' a flood of sunrays that shined from behind my head. He squinted in the sunlight and I decided to go easy on him.

"You know, Mr. Jasper," I started gently; "I am the fifth consecutive generation of professional women in my family. The first-generation American was the niece of Umbatala, crowned prince of the Niger. Without the benefit of the spoken language on the plantation, she escaped the sellin' block and grew up free among her people on an island off the coast of South Carolina. She migrated to Granville where she managed an entire house staff and was in charge of buyin' and sellin' the farm animals. The only duty she did not govern on the whole plantation was the supervision of the field hands. My mother is a teacher at the church school and everyone knows Mama Tutu was the wealthy heir of a judge in Fort Hunt, Virginia. I do not know what it means to take orders unless it is part of a trainin' experience that I need to learn how to teach others. I'm sure you can understand this, am I right, Mr. Jasper?"

At this point Jasper Ale began getting irritated. "Yes, ma'am I reckon I do. But that don't seem to give me much in line of the kind of information I was afta'. Let me put it to you plain like," he said. "Is Mr. Washington comin' back?"

"I'm talkin' about you. How you have treated me and how you continue to think you have some authority over me."

"I should have never gave you up. I would have kept you in your place. I told you I was willin' to keep my silence, but you pushin' me now, miss."

"Silence about what, pray tell?"

I looked sternly into the eyes of my old teacher. The one who had once said I would never be accepted into the Normal School. The one who had laughed and jeered instead of promoted and cheered me toward my goal—a goal now attained without his help. My life goal was affirmed and supported by only one other person outside of myself and Mama Tutu. And who was that? Mr. Washington! The man I cherish and love more than a husband, brother or father because of his undyin' faith in me. His belief that I would continue his legacy has been more than enough to keep me goin'.

By this time Mr. Jasper had run out of patience. He raised his cane and pointed it disrespectfully toward me.

"You needed him, and you know why?"

But before he could finish, I answered, "Because he could see me for who I was, not like you who only saw what you didn't want me to be."

"What I wanted you to be was who you were."

"And who was that, Mr. Jasper Ale?"

"My chile."

"Your what?"

"Yes, that's right. You are not Judd Outlaw's chile. You mine. But no, I did-n't have enough money and Judd Outlaw was picked to be your mama's husband 'cause Mama Tutu didn't think I was good enough. And what I always wanted you to be was who you were."

Shocked at this disclosure, I replied with the news he had come to find.

"The letter says he's too ill to move."

"What the dickens are you made of, gal? Did you hear what I just said?"

"Mr. Washington is too ill to move," I replied. "Which means I'm in charge of the school now and he ain't comin' back. Which news do you think concerns me most?"

"Lawd have mercy," he cried out.

His head dropped down upon the frail hands back restin' on the cane. A thick and mournful silence filled the whole room.

"What do we do now, chile?" he asked.

This was the first time I had ever heard a tone of endearment in that old man's voice. He barely lifted his head. It was obvious that he was tired. His strength seemed to drain out from his body through the sadness in his eyes. I saw deeply into the windows of his soul and spoke directly to his heart's question.

"Mr. Washington left provisions for his work to continue when he left me in charge of the school and we will go on with his work uninterrupted. Although we will all be sad at his partin'," I continued, "I have beheld him as more than a father but also as one sees a comet passin'.

"Like a comet, another one won't come again for 70,000 years. We have all seen this one, this time, and he has certainly blazed the trail. I still remember the first time I saw him, sittin' high up in the saddle of his black stallion. The sun was glarin' in my eyes and I could only see his hair. He looked a thousand light years away when I looked up into his eyes through the strain of my childish squint, but at the same time he pierced my soul with his glance. It was then that I felt the radiance of his magnificence."

"You did need him. He did for you what I never could have done."

"I would say Mr. Jasper Ale, that is the first time you got your history facts right. So just keep your little news a secret between us and I won't hold you responsible for what you couldn't and didn't do."

Later that day the final news that came was that he had ridden into the sunset. The hour had come of the death of my longtime friend and mentor; I could not even respond. I couldn't even feel. A big cavity sat where my chest was supposed to be. I had known about his sickness from the time he was first diagnosed. He defiantly chose to ignore the warnin's. After he found out he was sick, he worked even harder to ensure that the work would not die with him. I tried to get him to slow down, but I knew it had been futile. It was his choice; if he was dyin', he would die of terminal exhaustion. I wanted to go to him, he wouldn't let me.

"Stay, Pansy, and see to the school," he ordered.

He needed to be rescued like a helpless cat at the end of a high tree limb. I couldn't leave my post, not even to visit him, because he was dependin' on me bein' at the school. I knew he was worried about the problems involvin' the entrance of new female students. The tension that had stirred up over havin' women students was increasin' and if I left there would be no one to quell the male students' uprisin'. I had hoped he would try harder to recover knowin' I needed him here. In my mind, heart and spirit, he would never die. I did need him. Death could visit but would not stay with him. I tried to convince myself that the news was just a warnin'. It was a way to scare him into comin' back.

Huckabuck Marie also came to visit me the minute she heard about the headmaster's health. She and I worked very diligently administerin' the institution. By the time I was appointed dean of students, Huckabuck Marie was the headmaster's office manager. Part of her duties was to keep the calendar for Mr. Washington. She confessed she had spent the last month rearrangin' his schedule in spite of the fact that there was still no sign of his return. She, like everyone else, expected him to be back long before now. She had to begin cancelin' appointments instead of reschedulin' them. I watched her as she approached the porch, holdin' her parasol down in front of her face. She doubled her pace as she drew nearer to the buildin'. She ascended the porch steps clingin' to the railin' and nearly stumblin' into the door that I pulled opened before she knocked. When she arrived, she was visibly shaken, entering the room without even noticing Jasper Ale. She practically collapsed in my arms and began to cry.

"Dearest," she said, trying to choke back the tears. "I have the worst sickly feeling about all this. It is totally irrational, isn't it? Please tell me it is."

"I wish I could," I replied, "but you know better than I do, Huck, that your feelin's don't tell no lies. It's not your job to change what you feel; now it's our job to deal with what it means."

"Oh, but this time I wish they would lie, just this once. I spent the whole mornin' cancelin' his engagements. I didn't know what to say. I have used all the excuses in the book already. I just say, he's been delayed indefinitely in Boston and as soon as he returns to his office I will notify them. What on earth is goin' on up North, Pansy? This is not like Mr. Washington, and this doesn't feel right. It just doesn't feel right at all."

Huckabuck Marie fell apart then. Cryin' and moanin' like the professional wailers in church. I tried to comfort her but she kept on sobbin'. I guided her over to the chaise lounge and sat her down. She was blind with grief. I sat by her side tryin' to figure out a way to be optimistic like I always had. I couldn't think of a thing to say. I rocked her in my arms until she quieted down and then the only thing I could think of doin' was to softly sing the same sweet melody that, in my childhood, always helped to calm my own fears.

"Oh my baby, my little baby. Oh my dahlin' sweet little girl. Sweet little, sweet little, sweet little girl. Strong and smarter than any in the world."

She calmed down feelin' the warmth and concern that I had felt so many times in the arms of Mama Tutu.

"Huck," I whispered.

"Shhh," was her response.

"But, Huck—"

"Shhh…shhh. Pansy, don't tell me, I can't stand to hear any bad news right now."

"You know already. I can tell, so don't let's hide the truth from each other," I pleaded. "I need you to be with me through this."

"What do you mean, go on tell me what's wrong?" asked Huckabuck Marie softly.

"A star is fallin' from heaven today, Huck, our star. In the descendin' flight he made the brightest shower of light. He'll leave a void that will be impossible to fill. The legacy and the traditions will be ours to uphold, you know."

"Oh no, Pansy, I can't hear it," she replied. "I wish I could wave a magic wand and erase the last year. Then it would take away the sadness of this heartrendin' day. Though if I could, we would have lost the joys of that year too."

"It's gonna be all right," I assured her.

Jasper Ale quietly slipped away and we were left alone to try to console each other. The late afternoon sun poured into the room and filled it with gentle warmth. I looked out into the metallic day and saw thousands of tiny air molecules dancin' in the sunlight. I blinked, squinted and then rubbed my eyes. The molecules were still there. I remembered Dr. Carver, not more than a few days before, tellin' me that the whole universe was composed of millions of tiny little molecules. The point was not any clearer then, than it was that day. Yet, these lively air-born bein's gave me a sense of community and a feelin' of not bein' alone.

"It's gonna take a mighty big foot to fit into his shoes."

"More than two sets of feet," Huckabuck Marie responded with a smile.

"I think he had it in mind for me to get married to Dr. Carver. I'll never quite know for sure, unless I see him again."

"Who wants to get married anyhow? I get a sweaty fever just thinkin' of it," answered Huckabuck Marie. "I ask you, Pansy Outlaw, what man is goin' to work for a woman who can work for herself? I tell you, it's not easy for a man to look in the face of an independent woman every day."

"If we don't get married, we'll be ruined, won't we?'

"If I did marry," said Huckabuck Marie, "that would be ruin for me and the groom. I can guarantee you that."

"What about our reputation, our heirs?" I asked.

"If we don't get married, we won't have heirs!" she said.

'Do you realize the only person who could help us solve this riddle?'

"Of course I do. I wish he was here."

I saw tears fall innocently from her eyes when she spoke.

"Correction," I said, "first of all, he is here, I can feel him strong, and, secondly, he never left Granville without placin' his total trust in us. This time is no exception. We've been through fire befo' and we been through rain. We've seen death come and go again. Huck, this time death is not in vain, and we'll get through this too, just the same."

Mr. Washington passed. His passin' had a severe impact on us both, we also both felt that somethin' magnificent had been discovered. Each of us had found ourselves, and with the death of our mentor had, at the same time, found each other. I sat thinkin' but nothin' that I could think right then was ever fully rational. The truth of the matter is that this faulty existence we call livin' has so many events that we cannot control and life is what happens in the process.

"You know death is more of life than life is life," I said.

"I don't understand a thing you sayin' but I do know one thing for sho', chile, you spend too much time explainin' death then I care to hear," Huckabuck Marie snipped.

The night he slipped away from time and his silent escape was broken by the sound of a rooster's crow. It was the break of day, marked by the domestic cock's call, which had always signaled the field workers to labor. This time it signaled our headmaster to rest. The crowin' startled Huckabuck Marie, who was more accustomed to livin' above the shops in town where mornin' didn't begin 'til afternoon.

She had fallen asleep and I let her rest. I was already busy workin' in my study on the letters regardin' the status of the school. In order to insure a smooth transition of authority, I had to provide detailed information to all the school's shareholders. I knew them all, and my challenge would be to convince them that I had what it took to administer the entire school operations. I was fumblin' through papers and deep in thought when Mama Tutu arrived. Her bangin' on the door was enough to wake the dead. Huckabuck Marie jolted awake in a quandary as to where she had spent the night.

"Funerals are what 'da good Lawd keeps me alive fo' nowadays," said Mama Tutu.

"I done buried mo' folks than Dr. Carver has peanuts. Buryin' Mr. Washington now that's gonna take some doin'. This is like havin' the life drain right out of me. Oh Lawd, we know you never make a mistake so show us the way to accept yo' will in our hearts. You gals may not know or believe this but a broken heart is twice as big as one that has no grief."

"Oh, Mama Tutu!" It was my turn to cry now and I completely broke down.

Mama Tutu held me in her arms while Huckabuck Marie fanned my wretched face totally distorted in hysterics. Not that I really wanted to know, I decided to ask Mama Tutu about what Jasper Ale had said.

"Mama Tutu?"

"Yes, darhlin'."

"Jasper Ale was here yesterday and he told me—"

She interrupted, "Don't mind anythin' that 'ole buzzard has to say. He like circlin' round a dead carcass hoping to feed his hunger. It's Mr. Washington needs our attention right now. Don't you agree?"

"Yes, ma'am. I just wanted to know if he is really—"

"I told you not to listen to that fool, now didn't I? Besides, tell me one thing that man eva' did but try to keep you barefoot and pregnant! You ain't lost your last mind, did ya?"

"No, ma'am," I answered humbly.

"Don't you remember about Lil' Luke? When we 'dopted him, he ain't eva' knowed his real pappy? Judd Outlaw bore his life and yours too. That's who a father is, and don't eva' forget that."

"Can't nobody take that away from him, and can't nobody take him away from you. That sorry 'ole Jasper Ale been tryin' to stop the hand of time all his life."

Then Huckabuck Marie had a question.

"Where do we go from here?" she asked.

"There's only one way to go, Huck," I answered regainin' my composure with Mama Tutu around, "and that's forward."

"Now let's open up the window and let them swingin' chariots leave us a cool breeze in their path," Mama Tutu proclaimed.

I needed a walk. I walked over to the lake on the other side of the school grounds, where the livestock was kept. The sultry August sun hung languidly in the afternoon over the lagoon. I needed some time alone and I was admittedly too big for the tree house. Confusion is tamed in solitude. I longed for summer constantly but winter came no matter how much I tried to resist it. Is summer endin', or is it winter beginnin'? I looked over the lagoon and wished it were the Dead Sea. I would've walked ceremoniously into it to find healin' for the wound that replaced the hole left by my ruptured heart. Instead, I returned to join Mama Tutu and Huckabuck Marie to share with them the pain of losin' him.

I sat starin' at the vast cultivated field from my dormitory window. "He will never die, and we will never die," I murmured. "Just like the fertile ground stretchin' onward through time, we will go on and on. Our fate is like the river that rises from the sea, descends on mountaintops, and journeys a lifetime back to the ocean. We will always return, for generations to come, for we are among the civilized blacks. Our soul is the ever expandin', part of an immortal spirit that will never die."

Luke finished his speech. He yelled down to his friend to come and hear it, but no one answered. When he came downstairs, my head was slumped across the dinin' room table. I was drunk from the revelries of the past.

"What's goin' on? Where is everybody? Aunt Pansy, you all right?" he asked as he tiptoed by the dinin' room doorway and scurried around to get his friend to help revive Aunt Pansy.

"I can't believe you," he said shakin' him awake, "a great legislative speech is born, and where are you? I find you sleepin' in the closet. Come on, Aunt Pansy's flat out across the table."

The two of them rushed into the dinin' room fearin' the worse.

I was just takin' a nap after the long journey back. First my chin was restin' on my chest like it was holdin' my head on a plate. Then I guess I got real comfortable and just spread out on the table. I musta been a sight, because they panicked.

"Aunt Pansy!" they screamed with trepidation. "Aunt Pansy, please! Wake up, please!"

"I'm all right. I'm all right." I repeated several times before they heard me. One was lookin' for the smellin' salts and the other was rushin' toward me with a cold towel.

"What's the matter with you young boys? Can't nobody take a little snooze once in a while?"

"Well. er...yeah well...we thought..." Luke tried to explain.

"No need to tell me what ya'll thought, I already know. With all them brains you got, you ought to be able to tell if someone is dead or alive.

"For the life of me, I just can't understand why you fussin' to be on that man's legislature anyhow. There's a world of difference between them and us. Like the good book says, 'I have been young, and now am old, yet have I not seen the righteous forsaken, nor his seed beggin' bread' and we'll die when we die and we'll never go beggin' long as we remember we's de Lawd's incomparable civilized blacks.'"

Epilogue

Josh went on to win the election. Pansy Outlaw nurtured the next generation of Outlaws. Huckabuck Marie worked in the school archives until she went blind and retired in her late eighties in a house built by Papa Judd on the Outlaw estate. Much of what is ours to tell we know because she kept such good records. The Normal School grew steadily under Pansy's leadership and is still flourishing.

One of my daughters wrote the poem that follows in 1989 when she was fourteen years old. It is more than one hundred years after the reconstruction and youth like Pansy Outlaw made the statement that, "I won't be no slave." Will this new generation have statements that make their life? As we remember from whence we have come, let us remember that we are not all descendants of slaves. I believe the following poem describes our best defense in the wake of consciousness. Let the bells of truth ring out in the land and the broken liberty forever stand as a reminder of the old world. We will always look back with pride. It is for the children that we live out our destiny.

VENGEANCE

It's a bittersweet taste
Dominating my brain,
Like a sweetly festering
Rotting sugar cane.

The drumming cruel beat
Pounds deep in my head
As mayhem constructs
And I lie dazed in bed.

How could they?
Why would they?
The questions I ask
No longer matter.

I must complete the task,
Divide and destroy
Like soldiers at war.
Vengeance be mine.
My soul's on the floor

The way from the start,
An eye for an eye,
A tooth for a tooth,
A cry for a cry.

Turn the other cheek?
Is it only for saints?
Are all humans alone
In sorrow's complaint?

In my right hand a rosary,
My left holds a knife.
Do I do as in heaven
Or as in earth and in life?

I must make the decision,
A final chapter I must write.
Do I stroll in the sunshine
Or stumble through night?

-Hasna Binta, 1989

CPSIA information can be obtained
at www.ICGtesting.com
Printed in the USA
BVHW031703191222
654561BV00013B/789